STARFORCE

on the

RISE

STEVE BEHLING

Los Angeles · New York

First Edition, February 2019
10 9 8 7 6 5 4 3 2 1
FAC-020093-18355
Printed in the United States of America

Designed by Kurt Hartman
Cover Illustration by Veronica Fish

Library of Congress Control Number: 2018954010
ISBN: 978-1-368-04696-1

Visit www.DisneyBooks.com
and www.Marvel.com

SUSTAINABLE FORESTRY INITIATIVE — Certified Sourcing
www.sfiprogram.org
SFI-00993

THIS LABEL APPLIES TO TEXT STOCK

THEN

CHAPTER 1

"All I'm saying is, the only reason we're in this mess is because of you, twinklefists."

Vers crouched down in the muck, her brown eyes boring a hole right through Minn-Erva's accusing glare. "Wait, what now? How is this my fault? And where do you even get off calling me 'twinklefists'?" Vers was so over Minn-Erva's cracks and sarcasm. No matter what she tried to do, she couldn't seem to gain the esteem of her fellow Kree Starforce warrior. Right now, she was done caring.

Minn-Erva's nose wrinkled slightly, and her upper lip twitched. It was clear to anyone who knew her even remotely that she had a lot to say, and it was about to come pouring out.

That's when the shooting started.

Or more accurately, that's when the shooting—which had pretty much been a constant since they had been discovered—cranked up a few hundred notches.

Minn-Erva yelled over the din of laser fire, "Based on our current situation, I think I'm well within my rights to call you 'twinkle-fists,'" then added almost as an afterthought, "or anything else I come up with."

Rolling her eyes and resisting a retort, Vers clawed her way up the muddy wall in front of her, climbing to the top of the dirt ditch that she and Minn-Erva had dived into just minutes before. As she peered over the edge, she saw them, roughly a hundred meters out—a hunting pack of eight Skrull warriors. They were armed to the teeth, each packing a rifle, a sidearm, and grenades. Above them, another Skrull aboard a hovercraft kept close watch.

Searing laser fire erupted from one of the Skrulls' rifles, and Vers managed to slip the blast by relinquishing her hold on the muddy ridge, falling down into the ditch below. To Minn-Erva, it seemed that Vers had ducked *before* the laser blast scorched the air above her head. She had hit the ground even before the sound of the blast could be heard. Minn-Erva had to hand it to her teammate—she might not like her, but the woman had incredible reflexes.

"How many up there now?" Minn-Erva said, ejecting a cartridge from her weapon. She reached for a magazine from her belt, flipped it end over end in her hand, and slammed it into the weapon's loading compartment. One second later, the weapon emitted a high-pitched whine, indicating that it was ready to be fired.

"Eight," Vers said. "Give or take."

"With more on the way," Minn-Erva added.

Vers nodded. "Undoubtedly."

"Hold on. Did . . . did we just agree on something?" Minn-Erva asked.

Vers cracked a grin. "Sadly, yes," she said. "Believe me, no one's more upset about it than I am."

CHAPTER 2

Less than an hour earlier, everything had been running like clockwork. Minn-Erva and Vers had entered the space surrounding Aphos Prime in a small, two-person Kree fighter. The ship's larger external weapons had been stripped in favor of adding an additional engine with enough thrust to enable the vessel to evade the Skrulls, who controlled the space surrounding Aphos Prime, as well as the planet itself.

Due to its incredible speed, the Kree fighter had managed to avoid detection. But in order to do that, the ship had to move faster than a normal spacecraft, and maintain that speed well into entry of Aphos Prime's atmosphere.

The fighter entered the upper atmosphere well above cruising speed. Normally, a vessel like theirs would have engaged reverse thrust to slow the ship down, before allowing the atmosphere to act as a kind of natural air brake. But Vers and Minn-Erva couldn't afford that luxury, unless they wanted to alert the Skrulls to their presence.

To say the Kree fighter took a beating upon entry was like saying that Minn-Erva and Vers didn't get along—pretty obvious, and a gross understatement. The ship bounced around on the atmosphere at first, and nearly threatened to skip right off and back into outer space. Vers stayed at the helm, riding the ship, fighting with the controls every step of the way.

"Yon-Rogg said this was gonna be easy, didn't he?" Minn-Erva shouted over the screaming engines. It sounded for all the world like the ship was going to shake itself apart.

"Uh-huh," Vers yelled back.

"You sure you know what you're doing?"

Minn-Erva asked skeptically, steadying herself in her seat.

"Of course I'm sure. I can fly anything," Vers said. She wasn't bragging; it was just a fact. Since she had joined Starforce, Vers had proven herself across numerous levels and disciplines. Everything from strategy to battlefield tactics, weapons and unarmed combat, ground-based and airborne vehicles. You name it, Vers was good at it.

Which kind of annoyed Minn-Erva.

The Kree fighter continued its assault on the atmosphere of Aphos Prime, piercing the planet's ozone layer. The hot gasses that had built up on the ship's underbelly were dissipating, and the hull sounded less like it was going to crumple or explode at any given moment.

It was time for Phase Two.

In order to avoid detection by the Skrulls' planetary sensors, Vers had to keep the thrusters pinned at faster-than-landing speeds. While this kept the Kree warriors safe from the threat of being blown up by their enemy, it made the

possibility that they would smash into the surface of Aphos Prime a very real one.

"Hang on," Vers said, as the ship bucked up
and down. "Landing in ten!"

"Ten?!" Minn-Erva protested. "There's no
way! We're going way too fast, you'll kill us!"

"Anything is possible," Vers muttered. Then,
in a more audible voice, "Hang on!"

As it turned out, not only was it possible, it
was the most likely outcome. The ship surely
would have exploded on impact, if Vers hadn't
engaged the ship's thrusters at the five-second
mark. Minn-Erva was thrown back against her
seat with significant force, to the point where
she thought she was going to be pushed right
through it.

Then she felt her stomach hit her throat,
and it seemed as though the ship's bottom was
going to give way.

The vessel skimmed the planet's surface,
hitting the ground, then popping up, like

a rock skipping along the surface of a lake. Every time the craft went up, Vers shoved the controls forward, tilting the ship's nose back down. Then it would hit the ground once more, and bounce upward again. The pattern continued for several seconds, until the ship's momentum was at last depleted, and the vessel came to a sputtering rest in a mudbank.

"At least we're not dead," Minn-Erva said sarcastically, as she unstrapped herself from her seat.

Vers was right behind her. " 'Wow, that was a great landing, Vers. I can't imagine anyone else being able to pull that off,' " she prompted helpfully.

"What, you want me to say thank you? Really?" Minn-Erva grumbled, as she went to the weapons rack on the wall. She lifted her rifle, an ammunition belt, and a sidearm. Vers met her there, and took the same weapons.

"For protection and defense only, Vers," Minn-Erva clarified with a look. "Remember what Yon-Rogg said."

"Got it, Mom," Vers replied sarcastically as she strapped on the weapons. "And I'm just saying, a thank-you wouldn't be out of the question," Vers said.

"I am not saying thank you," Minn-Erva declared with finality. "Not now, not ever."

"Bet you do," Vers replied.

When Minn-Erva said nothing, Vers kept talking. "I'm serious. Before this mission is over, I bet you thank me."

"You must like losing" was all Minn-Erva could say as she stomped toward the ship's exit hatch.

CHAPTER 3

They weren't even a minute into the mission briefing before Vers was asking questions. It had all started promisingly enough. Within the confines of the stuffy briefing room, Yon-Rogg, commander of Starforce, had gathered Minn-Erva and Vers to walk them through a two-person mission.

The action on Aphos Prime was supposed to be easy. A "no-brainer," as Vers would have described it—one of her odd expressions that her teammates shrugged off as Vers being, well, Vers. Yon-Rogg had actually described it as a "routine reconnaissance mission." A Kree scout ship had reported Skrull activity on a remote planet, Aphos Prime. The ship had

13

managed to get off one communication before the vessel was destroyed by enemy fire.

"Any survivors?" Vers asked.

"No," Yon-Rogg replied, his voice dispassionate. "The Skrulls don't leave witnesses. Therefore, your mission is simple. You will touch down on Aphos Prime undetected. You will ascertain the strength of the Skrull force encamped on the planet, and you will report back, so we can plan further action."

"Report back?" Vers asked.

"Yes," Yon-Rogg said, prepared for resistance. "Report only. You are not to engage the enemy."

"Well, *we* might not engage the enemy, but they're sure as heck gonna engage *us*," Vers said aggressively.

"Vers . . ." Yon-Rogg interjected.

"Why send members of Starforce on a job like this, anyway?" Vers asked. "If it's just a straightforward recon mission, why bring us in? It doesn't make sense."

"I wasn't aware we were questioning orders,"

Minn-Erva said, her voice drenched in sarcasm. "Or did I miss that part of the briefing?"

"I'm not questioning the order," Vers said, a little defensively. "I'm just saying. We're warriors. Fighters. We're not scouts. Not me. Not with these." Vers raised both hands in front of her, indicating the photon blasts that could erupt from her fingertips at a moment's notice.

Minn-Erva was about to say something else, when Yon-Rogg cleared his throat. Whatever she was going to say, Minn-Erva suddenly thought better of it.

"The order comes from the Supreme Intelligence," Yon-Rogg said, ending any further discussion of the matter.

Vers nodded. "Understood," she said.

But all three of them knew she didn't mean it.

In the hallway outside the briefing chamber, Vers watched as Minn-Erva strode ahead, the sniper rifle she wore strapped across her back like a second skin. Since joining Starforce, Minn-Erva had been the most difficult member for Vers to form even a tentative connection with, let alone truly befriend. Att-Lass, Korath, Bron-Char—they each came with their own quirks, but they seemed to appreciate Vers for who she was and welcome her as a valuable addition to the team.

Minn-Erva, not so much.

A moment later, she felt a presence behind her. She turned, and saw Yon-Rogg.

"I'm sorry," Vers said, trying to make her tone sound genuinely contrite. "I shouldn't have questioned the order."

Yon-Rogg shook his head. "You are a good warrior, Vers," he began. "You have the potential to become a great one. But you must learn that every warrior has their place. And yours is not to question. Ours is not to question. Ours is to follow the orders of the Supreme Intelligence. For the good of the Kree Empire."

"For the good of the Empire," Vers repeated, casting her eyes downward.

"This mission is more important than you know," Yon-Rogg added. "It's vital that we determine the exact strength of the Skrull force on Aphos Prime."

"Why are we so concerned about their numbers?" Vers asked. "Shouldn't we want to know what it is that they're doing, more so than how many are doing it? Or even better, stop them from doing it altogether?"

"That will come," Yon-Rogg said. "Consider this a test."

"A test?" Vers echoed as Yon-Rogg walked away.

It took her a few seconds, but then it clicked. "You're testing me and Minn-Erva, aren't you?" Vers said, loudly, to Yon-Rogg's rapidly shrinking figure.

"I'm not answering," he replied over his shoulder.

"I knew it!" Vers shouted.

As Yon-Rogg reached the end of the hall-way, the yellow elevator doors slid open. He stepped inside, and turned around to face Vers as the doors closed. Maybe it was her imagination, but she could have sworn there was the slightest hint of a smile on his stern face.

CHAPTER 4

"You know, some people might say it's a sign of intelligence to check a planet's atmosphere before they open the hatch and expose themselves and members of their team to a potentially toxic environment," Vers said, glaring at Minn-Erva.

Her teammate had simply opened the hatch door without performing any of the routine atmospheric checks. Granted, Aphos Prime was a known entity. It had been charted previously, and Kree probes revealed the planet had a breathable atmosphere similar to their home world. But who knew what could have happened since the Skrull enemy had taken up residence on the planet?

Vers was annoyed. Usually, she was the one who would subvert protocol. She wasn't sure how she felt about someone else on the team copying her act.

"Are you coming?" Minn-Erva asked, ignoring Vers's comment and making her way out the hatch.

"Right behind you," Vers called out, as she was just about to jump.

From outside the ship, Vers heard Minn-Erva say, "Then you'll want to watch your—"

Vers threw herself from the hatch, and promptly landed stomach-first in a muddy field, making an unsavory squelching sound.

"—step."

Vers stood and looked down with distaste. She was now covered in mud from head to toe. Then she looked at Minn-Erva, and saw that the same thing had happened to her when she'd exited the ship.

"Natural camouflage," Vers offered.

Minn-Erva didn't laugh.

"What are the odds of us having arrived without tripping any Skrull alarms?" Vers asked.

"We came in fast and hot," Minn-Erva said, scraping mud from a disc-shaped device she clutched in her right hand. "No way they could have gotten a bead on us. If their scanners picked up anything, they would have us pegged for a meteorite. There's a lot of that kind of activity in this sector."

"That *almost* sounded like a thank-you," Vers said.

"You wish," Minn-Erva shot back, her gaze still locked on the object in her hand. Shaking it several times, Minn-Erva sighed. "There's something wrong with this."

Vers took a step toward Minn-Erva and looked over her shoulder. The device that Minn-Erva held was a delicate tracking system that could detect the Skrulls' unique DNA signatures.

"What's wrong with it?" Vers asked.

"When I first tried to activate it, the tracker

went haywire," Minn-Erva said, shaking her head. "Now, there's nothing. Must be some kind of interference."

"You think it's being jammed?" Vers asked.

"No way," Minn-Erva said. "They'd have to know we were here."

"Uh-huh," Vers said. "So . . . what if they know we're here?"

"I thought you were such a great pilot that they'd never know we were coming." Minn-Erva looked at her with a smirk. "So how could they know?"

"Good point," Vers said.

Suddenly, the tracker came to life again, flashing in the palm of Minn-Erva's hand. "We have signals," Minn-Erva said, her voice tense. "Multiple targets. That direction." She nodded her head to the east. Then the tracker went dark once more.

"There must be something about the planet itself that's playing havoc with the tracker," Vers mused.

"Great," Minn-Erva replied. "Mission's off to a good start."

With that, Vers touched a control on her left glove. The Kree fighter, half-buried in the mud, briefly shimmered, until it disappeared completely from view. "Ship's cloaked," she said. "Let's move. At least we have a direction. If we stay here, we're sitting ducks out in the open."

"What on Hala is a 'sitting duck'?" Minn-Erva asked. "Never mind—I don't want to know."

✳

"Anything?"

Minn-Erva looked at the tracker. It had flashed bright red a few minutes earlier, then the blips faded from sight. The signal confirmed that they were at least on the right path, but it didn't last long enough to provide an accurate count of the Skrull forces that occupied the planet.

"Not since the last blip," Minn-Erva replied.

"Maybe if we get close enough to the source, we can get a read."

"At this point, we're going to be giving Yon-Rogg a visual confirmation of the numbers," Vers said. "And we're going to have to engage the enemy if we get that close. You know it, I know it. There's no way around it."

"Are you pushing for a fight, is that it?" Minn-Erva said. "You always have to push it too far, Vers. Don't even think about it. You heard Yon-Rogg. Do not engage."

Vers grumbled to herself as the duo continued to trudge along a muddy ravine. As Vers walked, she heard a *SCHLORP* sound every time a boot went into the mud, and a *THWUCK* sound every time one came out, each sucking noise serving as a punctuation to the angry thoughts bouncing around her head. Who had died and made Minn-Erva the boss? Where did she get off, parroting Yon-Rogg and trying to tell Vers what to do?

Finally, Vers couldn't take it any longer. She had to say what was on her mind.

"Question," Vers said, and as she turned her head to look at her comrade, she could see Minn-Erva already rolling her eyes. "Why don't you like me?" Vers hated that it made her sound like she cared, even a little. But she was genuinely curious. What was it about her that set Minn-Erva so on edge?

Minn-Erva looked at Vers for a moment, incredulous. "*Like* you? What are we, children?"

Now it was Vers's turn to roll her eyes. "Look," she said, taking another step in the mud.

SCHLORP.

"No," Minn-Erva said, whirling around, finger in Vers's face. "*You* look. You do what you do, and I get it. You're an asset. Yon-Rogg thinks you have something to offer Starforce. So does the Supreme Intelligence."

"And you?" Vers asked, pointedly.

Minn-Erva didn't say anything for a moment. Then, slowly, "I think you make a lot of noise. I think you cause a lot of damage. I think you don't have any control. And that makes you a danger. To me, to the team, even to yourself. You keep a lid on it, follow my lead, and maybe we'll make it off this mudball."

Then Minn-Erva turned around without another word and continued ahead through the filthy surface.

SCHLORP.

THWUCK.

"Right," Vers said to her teammate's retreating back. "Good talk."

CHAPTER 5

An hour had passed since Vers and Minn-Erva had last spoken. After their confrontation in the ravine, neither had tried to spark conversation with the other. They continued to wade through the mud in silence, looking for occasional signs of life from the tracker that Minn-Erva clutched in her right hand.

SCHLORP.

THWUCK.

SCHLORP.

THWUCK.

The sounds had become monotonous, just like everything else on this planet, Vers thought. So far, it appeared the only thing that Aphos Prime seemed to have in abundance was mud, muck, and filth, and not in any particular order. The Kree probes had unearthed no natural resources of value, and no signs of life. Aphos Prime really was what it appeared to be—a big, rotating ball of mud.

Why the Skrulls would have any interest in a place like this was a mystery. Aphos Prime was too remote to be of any strategic value. It didn't border Kree territory. The surface was too unstable to provide a permanent base for troops, and it was useless as a port or refueling station for Skrull spacecraft.

So why?

That was the question that Vers kept rolling over in her mind, but the answer evaded her.

SCHLORP.

THWUCK.

"Quiet," Minn-Erva hissed, breaking the silence.

Vers suddenly sprang to attention, and looked at the tracker in Minn-Erva's hand. The dial had lit up again, displaying multiple red targets. Vers counted them quickly, before the dial faded.

Three.

Three Skrulls, within range, which meant they were within five hundred meters or so. Vers looked all around her, in front, behind, to the sides.

She couldn't see anything except mud.

Minn-Erva motioned for Vers to kneel down next to her. The two were close to the ground as she whispered, "I don't know if we have the drop on them, or they have the drop on us."

"That's not a good feeling," Vers said back.

Minn-Erva nodded. "This tracker is useless. There's no way we can get an accurate read."

"We're gonna have to go with visual contact," Vers said.

"Visual contact means fighting," Minn-Erva replied. "That's outside mission parameters."

"Mission parameters just changed," Vers said.

Minn-Erva paused, then sighed. "I believe they did," she finally answered.

✳

Army crawling along the muddy ground, Vers dragged her body up a hill. Her foot slipped in the slimy muck, and she very nearly fell into a trench that had worn into the hillside. With a grunt, she hefted herself up, and continued the slog.

Soon, she reached the top of the hill, and stretched her neck outward to get a good look at the enemy.

There were three of them, crawling through the mud, just as Vers had been doing. They appeared atop a hill roughly a hundred or so meters away. She was just about to slide back down the hill to alert Minn-Erva, when she heard one of the Skrulls shout, "Target acquired!"

Figures, Vers thought. The resounding blast from the Skrulls came as she released her tentative hold on the muddy surface, and immediately slid downward. She landed right in the trench, and saw Minn-Erva standing there, waiting.

She looked annoyed.

"Stealthy," Minn-Erva commented.

"Not in the mood," Vers replied.

"Moot point, they know we're here, and they know where we are," Minn-Erva reprimanded.

"And we know they're here, and where they are," Vers pointed out.

Minn-Erva looked worried. "What do you have in mind?"

"I think we might be able to scare them off," Vers said, raising her right fist.

"Stow that," Minn-Erva said. "It's too much, too fast, Vers. Yon-Rogg would not approve."

Vers smiled. "Yon-Rogg's not here."

The photon battery at the base of her neck had become a part of her. At times it emitted sensations or vibrations, but it was more of a continuous presence, almost soothing in its consistency. There were times that Vers even forgot that it was there. Not often, but sometimes.

This wasn't one of them.

Already, the familiar buzzing sensation sounded in her ears, and the hair on the back of her neck stood on end. Peeking her head over the hilltop, she saw the Skrulls, rifles ready. They opened fire. The blasts whizzed past Vers's head.

Vers stood to her full height. She balled each hand into a fist, arms stretched outward, toward the Skrulls. The buzzing sound in her ears continued to build, and her fists started to glow.

Photon energy erupted from her hands, and the beam sliced through the air, covering the distance between her and the Skrulls' hilltop in a nanosecond. The ground crystalized where the photon blast struck, making a hole about three meters across, sending the Skrulls flying.

She saw one of them try to regain his footing,

aiming a rifle at her. Vers raised her hands, and sent another burst his way.

There was a smoldering hole where the Skrull had stood.

Vers kneeled and slid back into the trench.

"I think that did it," Vers said confidently.

"You get them all?" Minn-Erva asked.

"One for sure," Vers said, taking a deep breath. Whenever she used her abilities, she felt a strange emptiness afterward. Like she needed to recharge. "But I'm betting the others will think twice before attacking us again."

Minn-Erva nodded.

Then, a soft humming noise sounded in the distance. Vers perked her ears up, looking toward the hilltop. The sound grew louder, the hum closer. She and Minn-Erva raised their eyes skyward, and they saw it.

A Skrull hovercraft, high above. In perfect position to fire on them.

"So much for thinking twice, twinklefists," Minn-Erva said.

CHAPTER 6

"How many up there now?" Minn-Erva said, ejecting a cartridge from her weapon. She reached for a magazine from her belt, flipped it end over end in her hand, and slammed it into the weapon's loading compartment. One second later, the weapon emitted a high-pitched whine, indicating that it was ready to be fired.

"Eight," Vers said. "Give or take."

"With more on the way," Minn-Erva added.

Vers nodded. "Undoubtedly."

"Hold on. Did . . . did we just agree on something?" Minn-Erva asked.

Vers cracked a grin. "Sadly, yes," she said. "Believe me, no one's more upset about it than I am."

"I'm definitely more upset," Minn-Erva said, hoisting her weapon.

"Now that we've established that," Vers said, "what's our next move? They've got us covered from above. I can take them out, but I need you to cover me. There are eight Skrulls on that ridge that are dying to take a shot at me."

"I know how they feel," Minn-Erva said, and Vers wasn't fully certain if she was joking or not. Then she took a deep breath, slung her rifle over her shoulder, and scrambled up the muddy hillside. "I've got your back," she said. "You take out that hovercraft."

"I'm on it," Vers said, as she dug her hands once more into the muddy wall before her.

When she reached the top of the hill, the Skrull hovercraft swung around. From her position, Vers could see the pilot catch a glimpse of her and bark commands into his communicator. She doubted he was telling his fellow Skrulls to invite her and Minn-Erva over for dinner.

Minn-Erva was already at her vantage point atop the hill, and laying down suppressing fire with her rifle. It was one against eight, and Minn-Erva was winning. Every time a Skrull sniper tried to squeeze off a shot to take out Vers, Minn-Erva responded with a burst that caused the sniper to duck. The volley was unceasing. The time between Minn-Erva's shots was practically nonexistent.

Which opened a window for Vers to unleash another blast of photon energy. She heard the buzzing sound in her ears again, the build, and the release. This one seared the air itself, leaving a stench of ozone in its wake. The beam extended upward from her fists to the Skrull hovercraft above, punching a hole right through the hull.

The blast soon enveloped the hovercraft. There was no explosion. In a matter of two seconds, the hovercraft simply ceased to be. Its pilot had thrown himself out of the ship right before, dropping twenty meters into the soft mud below.

"Hovercraft down!" Vers shouted.

"Great," Minn-Erva said, still squeezing off shots. While Vers had been busy taking out the hovercraft, Minn-Erva had brought down three Skrull snipers. "Then you can help me out here."

Vers turned toward Minn-Erva, and felt light-headed. She had used her powers again, before allowing herself sufficient time to recharge. Rather than risk another beam and further weaken herself, she grabbed for the sidearm that she had taken from the ship, threw herself to the muddy surface, and crawled over next to Minn-Erva.

"What, no more 'twinklefists'?" Minn-Erva asked sarcastically.

"I thought you didn't want me to use 'em in the first place," Vers said.

Minn-Erva was silent, then, "Like you said; Yon-Rogg isn't here."

Vers smiled as she aimed the weapon in her hand and fired at the remaining Skrulls.

"We need to get around this hill and get

behind them," Minn-Erva instructed. "That's the only way we're going to end this. Right now, it's trench warfare."

"I can keep them pinned down while you sneak around," Vers offered.

Minn-Erva shook her head. "I'm a sniper. And a better shot. No offense," she added half-heartedly.

Vers stared at Minn-Erva. "You totally meant offense."

"You're right, I did," Minn-Erva replied. "Truth hurts."

Vers wasn't offended—Minn-Erva's strongest assets were her undeniable instinct and ability as a sharpshooter. She was the best on Starforce, and right now she was the one best suited to keeping the Skrulls busy while Vers made her way around and took the enemy by surprise from behind. But the battlefield was wide-open. How could Vers get behind them without being seen?

SCHLORP.

Vers and Minn-Erva both turned at the

sudden sound. They peered behind them, but saw nothing.

THWUCK.

SCHLORP.

THWUCK.

Footsteps?

But where were they coming from? There was no one to be seen anywhere close to them, only the Skrull snipers on the opposite hill.

SCHLORP.

THWUCK.

The sounds were growing closer, as the mud all around them began to bubble.

What was happening?

CHAPTER 7

The mud around them, bubbling.

The stench of gas released with each pop, filling the air with the odious smell of sulfur.

The sickening sounds of something struggling to break free of the muck.

And then, at last, Vers saw it.

A little speck of green, just breaking the surface of the mud, right next to her. It was rounded and smooth, and as it issued from the muck, Vers wondered what it was, curiosity temporarily getting the better of surprise and fear.

The object protruded farther and farther from the mud, assuming a more distinctive shape until Vers and Minn-Erva could see the *thing* in its entirety.

It was a Skrull head.

Its eyes looked lifeless, its jaw opened in a silent scream, and for a moment, Vers thought that the Skrull was actually dead. But suddenly, the alien gasped for air, and attempted to reach for Vers. It grabbed her right leg, clawing desperately at her uniform.

"Save me! Save me!" the Skrull croaked, its voice a weak whisper.

Momentarily startled, Vers lurched back, breaking the Skrull's feeble grasp.

Then, just as quickly as the Skrull had appeared, it was sucked back under the mud with a disgusting *SCHLORP*.

The two members of Starforce stared at each other wordlessly, stunned into silence, as if to say, *What did we just see?*

Neither of them had an answer.

Suddenly, in the distance, they heard more screams, and they knew instantly where they were coming from.

Skrulls, as they were sucked beneath the muck-ridden surface of Aphos Prime.

"We need to get off this mudball," Vers said. "Now."

"I don't disagree," Minn-Erva allowed.

The two warriors let go of their purchase on the muddy hill and slid down its side. Along the way, they noticed the ground bubbling, little pockets of gas bursting through the mud. When they hit the bottom, they started their slog through the mud field, toward the ravine, and—hopefully—back to their ship. They had no idea if it was even functional at this point, but it was the only option.

"What do you think the Skrulls want with a planet that kills everything that lands on it, including themselves?" Vers asked.

"The same thing the Kree would want with it," Minn-Erva said. "It's a weapon."

"How do you make a weapon out of a planet?" By now, the women were practically hip-deep in mud as they waded across the field. Every step seemed to bring them just a little deeper into the muck, the level of mud creeping up their bodies slowly.

Minn-Erva had no answer.

Instead, the mud all around them seemed to reply. It bubbled, as it had before when the head of the Skrull broke through its surface. Vers and Minn-Erva stopped in their tracks. The mud continued to bubble, almost like it was boiling. The little pockets of gas popped when they hit the air, and once again, everything around them stunk of sulfur.

There was a low rumbling, as the mud started to roil and foam.

"I don't think this is mud . . ." Vers said, her voice trailing off.

"Then what is it?" Minn-Erva asked.

"Whatever it is," Vers said, "I think it's . . . alive."

CHAPTER 8

Vers had hardly spoken the words before the ground beneath her began to shift, sliding, the dark muck slowly creeping up her legs. She tried to pull herself free, but found it impossible. Glancing sharply at Minn-Erva, she saw the same thing happening to her teammate.

"What is this?" Minn-Erva shouted, struggling to free her legs in vain.

"Some kind of defense mechanism, maybe," Vers said.

"Fine. Let's give it something to defend against," Minn-Erva snapped, and pointed the weapon that was still in her hands toward the mud below. She fired a quick burst, and the ground began to rumble. The gas bubbles that had been percolating now came even faster, breaking through the skin of mud, popping, and filling the air with its noxious smell.

"I think you made it angry," Vers said, and she was right. The goop that had started to creep up Minn-Erva's legs now began to pull her downward into the mud itself, exerting more force than she could push against. Minn-Erva began to sink deeper into the surface of the planet.

"Give me your hand!" Vers shouted, reaching out, trying to grab Minn-Erva. But she was too far away, and disappearing fast.

"Can't . . . reach!" Minn-Erva yelled, struggling to meet Vers's extended hand. The mud was now chest-deep. Another second, and she was in up to her neck.

Vers's situation wasn't much better. The mucky substance had started to pull her into the ground as well, but so far only to her waist. She wondered for a moment if maybe

Minn-Erva's blast really had angered whatever this thing was, and that's why she was sinking faster.

She didn't have much time to think, though. Looking over at Minn-Erva, she saw her teammate's face poking out just above the mud's surface, her mouth slightly open in a terrified O.

Minn-Erva didn't say a word as she completely disappeared from sight.

Vers's instinct was to blast the ground with her photon abilities, but she instantly thought better of it. She remembered the way the mud had reacted when she fired at the Skrulls, how she had left a burning, gaping hole in the hill. Firing away at the mud wasn't going to get Minn-Erva back, and it wouldn't help her to free herself—it would destroy them both. Besides, she was weakened after expending so much energy earlier. Until she built her reserves back up, her powers would be useless.

Then it hit her. The way the Skrull had

appeared from the muck below, seemingly from out of nowhere, then disappeared.

Maybe there was something down there . . . ?

There was only one way to find out. Vers set to fighting against the muck, as hard as she could. Instantly, the ground around her reacted, exerting a strong counter-pull to her push, and she began to sink faster, faster. The mud rose to her chest, then to her neck. The suction on her feet was incredible. Even with her great strength, she couldn't seem to break free.

Which was just as well. She didn't want to.

Another few seconds, and the mud framed her face. Vers was gasping for air as she was about to go under completely.

Let's hope I'm right, she thought, right before the mud closed over her.

"Your foot is on my head."

Vers tried to open her eyes, but couldn't.

She brought a hand to her face, and rubbed away a layer of encrusted mud. Slowly, she looked around, blinking rapidly.

She appeared to be in some sort of tiny, muddy cavern, almost like a pocket of some kind. Vers was on her back, and as she lifted her head, she saw that her foot was indeed resting on top of someone else's head.

Minn-Erva's, to be exact.

"You can take it off now, before I shoot it off," Minn-Erva offered.

Vers moved her foot, resting it on the mud next to Minn-Erva. "How long have I been out?"

"No idea," Minn-Erva said. "I came to right before you did."

Minn-Erva grasped the sidearm in her right hand, and pressed a small button on its side, activating the weapon's targeting laser. It provided just enough light for the two women to see more of their surroundings. The pocket was caked in mud, just as the surface had been. But down here, there appeared to be vines embedded in the walls and the floor.

Vers put her hand to the ground, and felt that the vines were moving. Or rather, they were pulsing. One second, they were motionless. The next, they jumped slightly. This rhythm repeated itself, over and over.

Mud dripped from the pocket's ceiling, which Vers guessed was a little over a meter tall. Both she and Minn-Erva could sit up, but they couldn't stand. At best, they'd be able to crouch. But that wasn't their biggest concern at the moment.

"How are we still breathing?" Vers asked.

Minn-Erva looked around, then stared at Vers. "Better question: *Why* are we still breathing?"

Those are both equally good questions, Vers thought to herself in defense, *but fine.* "Whatever this thing is, it didn't want to kill us. It's providing us with oxygen, somehow." She looked at the ground again, and felt the vines pulse under her hands once more.

"I don't think these are vines at all," Vers

said. "They're like blood vessels, or some kind of respiratory system."

"So you're a scientist now?" Minn-Erva asked, shifting her weight from one foot to the other. The quarters were close and cramped, and it was difficult to stay in a crouched position without toppling over.

Mud dripped onto Vers's face. It barely registered. "We're gonna have to work together if we're gonna get out of here," Vers said.

Minn-Erva nodded. "You mean all of us?" she said.

Vers looked at her, confused. Minn-Erva nudged her head toward the space over Vers's shoulder. "We've got company."

Vers turned to see a distinctly green head slowly emerging from the muddy wall behind her.

CHAPTER 9

"You even *think* about moving, and your head is gonna look like Xandarian cheese."

Minn-Erva's weapon was pointed directly at the Skrull, who had sprouted from the muck only a moment ago.

"What brings you here, stranger?" Vers said, pointing a fist toward the Skrull.

"Please," the Skrull begged, gasping for breath. "I cannot fight. I am wounded. Pull me out of this filth, save me, please."

Vers and Minn-Erva exchanged looks. Their impulse was to blast the Skrull without a moment's thought, of course. They were Kree. They were warriors. They were Starforce. It was their sworn duty to protect the Kree

Empire. And that meant killing Skrulls.

But this was an extraordinary situation. In this case, they had to consider the possibility that taking out the Skrull might not be the wisest move at the moment. The Skrull could have valuable information. He might be able to tell them everything he knew, if he was to be brought back to Hala. Plus, the Skrull had managed to worm his way out of whatever pocket he had been imprisoned in. He might be an asset to Vers and Minn-Erva in escaping this nightmare.

Minn-Erva gave Vers a slight nod, and Vers understood her meaning. "You so much as blink, and you're toast," Vers said as she grabbed the Skrull's head, and started none too gently to pull him free from the muck wall.

"I don't know what 'toast' is," Minn-Erva said to the Skrull, "but if I were you, I wouldn't want to be it."

"I believe you," the Skrull replied. "Disgusting creatures."

He was now about half-inside the pocket,

and Minn-Erva helped Vers pull him in all the way. Even though he was lying down on his side, Vers could tell that the Skrull was relatively short, even for a Skrull.

"Now, I believe my comrade asked you a question," Minn-Erva said. "What are you doing here, Skrull?"

The alien seemed to be having difficulty breathing. He was wheezing with each labored inhale. Vers guessed that one of his lungs may have been punctured. Still, he tried to speak. "I will tell you nothing, Kree," the Skrull said, venom in his voice replacing the pleading tone he'd assumed before Vers had pulled him from the wall.

"Sounds like you're having some difficulty breathing," Vers said. "Maybe operating on one lung. You do realize that you're probably dying, and it's two against one. Not real good odds."

"If the situation were reversed, I would have killed you already. You are weak," the Skrull spat.

Vers ignored the comment entirely. Instead,

a light bulb turned on inside her head. "Wait, I recognize you. You're the Skrull who popped up next to me. Up there," she said, jabbing a finger toward the ceiling. "On the surface."

The Skrull just stared at Vers.

Vers continued. "And I assume that, before you decided to make a miniature career of scaring people half to death by popping up out of muddy surfaces, you were trapped in a pocket similar to this one, right?"

Again, the Skrull just glared at the Kree warriors.

"You must want to live awful bad to put up such a struggle," Vers said. "So don't come at me like you're all big and tough, and you don't care, and won't tell us anything. I think you'll tell us whatever we want to know, if it means we help you get out of here."

Minn-Erva turned her head, looking at Vers.

"Help . . . him?" Minn-Erva said, practically laughing.

"He freed himself from one of these pockets," Vers said. "He made it to the surface once already. He even tore his way through all this muck and into this chamber. We can use someone like that."

The practicality of Vers's suggestion wasn't lost on Minn-Erva. She looked at her teammate for a moment, then leveled her weapon directly at the Skrull's chest. "The way I see it, you have a choice," Minn-Erva started. "Either you help us get out of here, or I puncture your other lung, and we leave you here forever."

"What's it gonna be, champ?" Vers asked. "Time's wasting."

"I hate you both," the Skrull wheezed.

"The feeling is mutual," Vers replied.

There was a brief moment of silence as the pocket shuddered. The walls started to vibrate, and little gas bubbles began to pop up along the surface.

"What was that?" Minn-Erva said, pointing at the wall.

"It is alive. This whole cursed planet. It is alive," the Skrull managed.

"Full offense, but I think we figured that out already, genius," Minn-Erva said.

The Skrull shook his head. "Not alive as we know it. It's more like . . . It's like a cancer. The entire planet."

"What do you mean, a cancer?" Vers asked.

Pausing for a moment, the Skrull tried to sit up. Vers grabbed his shoulders and propped him up against a wall. The Skrull looked at Vers like he wanted to throw up from their minimal contact.

"You're welcome," Vers said cheerfully.

The Skrull glowered, but at length he mustered enough breath to speak. "This planet is a living organism, but it's not an animal. It's more like a diseased cell."

"Are you saying that Aphos Prime has been a 'diseased cell' all along?" Minn-Erva asked.

"No," the Skrull said. "Not all along. Because this 'planet' is not Aphos Prime. It's what's left of Aphos Prime."

"What's *left* of Aphos Prime?" Vers said.

The Skrull nodded sharply, wincing in pain as he did.

Suddenly, it started to make sense. The way Yon-Rogg had offered so little information about the mission. Perhaps he—perhaps even the Supreme Intelligence—didn't know what had happened to Aphos Prime. Maybe the signs of Skrull activity, the Kree Scoutship that had been destroyed, all of it . . . maybe it had sent alarm bells sounding through the Kree high command. They knew that something had happened on Aphos Prime, but they didn't know what. And they didn't want to risk the entire Starforce team to find out. Hence the two-person scouting-only mission.

But did that mean that Vers and Minn-Erva's own commander had knowingly sent them into a potential death trap? Or had he been kept in the dark by his superiors?

Vers wasn't sure which answer was worse.

In that moment, Vers wasn't sure of anything.

CHAPTER 10

"How did Aphos Prime get this way?" Vers asked. "Did the Skrulls have a hand in this?"

The Skrull coughed, and Vers noticed flecks of dark green on his lips.

Internal bleeding, she thought.

"The Skrulls did not do this," he said, ruefully. "We are as in the dark as the Kree."

"Why don't I believe you?" Minn-Erva said, her finger still on the trigger of her sidearm.

"What you choose to believe or not believe is not my concern," the Skrull barked. "I am telling the truth." Then he started to cough again, and his knees came to his chest. More flecks of green appeared on his lips, and a thin trickle of green blood trailed down past his right nostril.

Vers sensed the urgency of the situation. They may not have much time left with the Skrull, and at the moment he looked like their only ticket out of this mudhole. "All right, we can talk when we get out of here, and off this miserable world," Vers said. "How do we tunnel out of here?"

The Skrull faded for a moment before coming around. "The walls . . . where they bubble . . . they seem to be weakest. You can claw your way through."

"Not through," Minn-Erva corrected. "Up."

"Then let's start clawing," Vers said. "You lead the way." She pointed at the Skrull. He was in no condition to be doing much of anything at the moment, but neither Vers nor Minn-Erva could trust him enough to turn their backs on him and let him follow. The Skrulls were known throughout the Kree Empire to be capable of great duplicity. For all they knew, the Skrull's injury was a sham to lower their guard.

"Very well," the Skrull croaked. He started

to claw at the bubbling, muddy wall. Sure enough, as he had said, his fingers sank into it, and soon, he was pulling his body into the wall itself.

Minn-Erva turned to Vers. "I'll go next. I don't want to let that Skrull out of my sight for even a second," she said. "You bring up the rear. Make sure we aren't being followed."

"Followed?" Vers said, looking around her as if to say, *Do you see anyone else here?*

Minn-Erva sighed impatiently. "This Skrull figured out how to survive down here. If he did, the others could have, too. I don't need them sneaking up on us, and taking us out one by one before we reach the surface."

"Good point," Vers admitted grudgingly. "But you didn't hear me say that."

The inside of the tunnel was illuminated by the laser sight from Minn-Erva's sidearm. Once they had breached the muddy wall of their pocket cell, the unlikely trio found themselves inside a slimy sort of tube, the Skrull breathing heavily from the exertion of their efforts thus far.

Vers worked out that the tube had to be a larger vine or blood vessel, like the ones that had lined the floor of the pocket they had just escaped from. The interior walls were dripping with mud, and there was a steady flow of the stuff directly beneath them as well. They were crouching, crawling through the vine, and the muck came up to their knees.

The Skrull was still leading the way, though his energy was clearly flagging. Vers figured they had gone twenty, maybe thirty meters into the vine. It seemed like they were heading up, toward the surface.

"I must . . . rest," the Skrull said, and he stopped crawling, promptly falling face-first into the muck on the ground. Minn-Erva yanked his head out of the grimy mess, and rolled him over. The Skrull was still breathing, but even more labored than before.

"He's not going to make it," Minn-Erva said.

"He has to," Vers replied. "We need him alive. We need him to talk to us. To Yon-Rogg. Otherwise this whole mission is a waste."

"Well then, I hope you're familiar with Skrull anatomy, Doctor," Minn-Erva said sarcastically.

Vers ignored Minn-Erva and darted over to the Skrull. Noticing the hole in his tunic, she grasped at the cloth and ripped it open, revealing a corresponding hole in his chest. It didn't look like a blaster wound. More like some kind of acid burn. She felt the air from the Skrull's lung whistling through.

Without pausing to think, Vers tore a piece of fabric from the Skrull's tunic and wadded it up into a ball. She stuffed the fabric into the hole in the Skrull's chest, trying to plug the hole and prevent the air from escaping. For a moment, the Skrull didn't react. Then his eyes went wide, and he rose with a start, coughing.

"Don't . . . touch me," the Skrull said, pushing Vers away.

"You're welcome," she replied. It was getting

to be a refrain, her performing tasks for people who just didn't seem to appreciate it, she thought ruefully.

Without another word, the Skrull got to his knees and started to crawl ahead once more.

Minn-Erva looked at Vers. "Well then, Doctor," she said. But her tone had a grudging respect to it that had been absent before the episode.

"You live long enough, you learn a few things," Vers said. Her tone conveyed a confidence that, at the moment, she didn't quite feel. The truth was, she wasn't sure how she knew what to do, and that troubled her. Emergency medical training certainly wasn't something she had learned under the tutelage of Starforce. Where had those instincts come from?

"Hala to Vers," Minn-Erva said. "We're leaving. You coming with?"

Vers shook the thoughts loose from her brain, snapping to attention, and, following Minn-Erva's crouched form, started to crawl.

CHAPTER 11

"I . . . I see something up ahead," the Skrull said, coughing.

Minn-Erva pushed the Skrull to the side. "What is that?"

Vers was bringing up the rear, and could only see her Starforce teammate and the Skrull immediately in front of her, obscuring her view. She glanced behind her, to make sure that no one—that no *thing*—was following them. *So far, so good.*

"What do you see?" Vers asked, her curiosity piqued.

"Get up here, Vers," Minn-Erva ordered. "Now."

The tunnel they were in was maybe about a

meter wide, give or take. Big enough that two people could fit side by side, but not three. Vers sidled up next to Minn-Erva.

Shoulder-to-shoulder with the sharpshooter, Vers looked ahead, past the Skrull who Minn-Erva still insisted on leading the trio. The laser sight on Minn-Erva's sidearm offered a little light, but not much. She could see that the vine they were in opened up into a larger cavern. It seemed to be filled with the same mud and muck that was running all along the floor of the tunnel.

But the strange part was that the cavern was filled from top to bottom with the muck so that it almost looked like an entirely solid wall. Yet, somehow, only a trickle of it was entering the tunnel where Vers, Minn-Erva, and the Skrull stood, mouths agape.

"How is that possible?" Vers asked, her voice quiet.

Minn-Erva shook her head. "You've got me."

Vers wiggled past the Skrull and over to the space where the tunnel met the cavern, and stretched out her hand. She found that there was some kind of membrane covering the opening. It felt wet and sticky, and moved like plastic when she pushed on it.

"What the heck is this place?" Minn-Erva said, sounding frustrated.

Vers looked upward and saw something even more remarkable. The mud that flowed throughout the cavern was dark, yet somehow translucent. She could see the surface of the planet at the top of the cavern, the signs of daylight unmistakable.

As was the bottom of the warriors' Kree fighter. There it was, free-floating in the surface muck.

All they had to do was get into the cavern, swim through the muck, and make their way to the ship. Then they were home free.

"All we have to do . . ." Vers began out loud, then paused, knowing it was much easier said than done.

"What's that?" Minn-Erva asked.

"Our ship," she said, pointing to the surface.

"It's right up there. If we can make it through this cavern and break through to the surface, we've got a chance of getting off this mudball."

"I have tried," the Skrull wheezed, clasping his chest wound with his left hand. "It . . . it isn't possible."

"Then why are you here?" Minn-Erva fired back.

"Because the other choice was . . . less attractive," the Skrull said, and Vers actually laughed.

"Are we ready to do this?" Minn-Erva asked, leveling her sidearm at the membrane.

Vers nodded. The Skrull nodded as well, though to be honest, neither Vers nor Minn-Erva cared very much whether the Skrull was ready or not.

"Count of three," Minn-Erva said. "One . . . two . . . three!"

She squeezed the trigger on her sidearm, and a blast of energy stabbed at the membrane. The force of the energy crackled against the membrane, and the tunnel rocked back and forth, shaking, knocking Minn-Erva backward.

Vers caught her as they both tumbled into the Skrull. They stared at the membrane.

It was still whole. The blast hadn't affected it in the slightest.

The same couldn't be said for the tunnel. All around them, the tunnel walls began to ooze more mud, and it was bubbling, as it had before. Except this time, vines were rising to the surface. They pulsed, and suddenly vines began erupting from the walls themselves.

"Watch out!" Vers yelled, ducking as one of the vines whipped around, narrowly missing her head. The vine slammed into the wall behind her, slicing right through it, as more thick mud poured out.

"It's trying to kill us!" the Skrull shouted.

"So, so obvious," Vers replied, as she pulled Minn-Erva out of the way of another vine. It narrowly missed Minn-Erva, but stabbed right into Vers's right thigh with a hiss. Vers felt white-hot pain for just a second as she grabbed the vine and threw it off. The place where it had touched her was now smoldering, like the vine was coated in some kind of acid.

The hole in the Skrull's chest, she thought.

More vines unfurled from the walls, and several wrapped themselves around the Skrull.

"Hey, twinklefists!" Minn-Erva shouted.

Vers spun around to face her teammate.

"Now would be a good time to blast something with those hands of yours," Minn-Erva said, squeezing off shots from her sidearm at the vines. Every one she hit, and she hit plenty, would split in half, spewing acidic liquid of some kind. But they were reproducing faster than she could take them out.

Vers looked down at her hands. She wasn't sure if she had recharged enough, but if she didn't use her powers now, they were as good as dead.

Or worse.

Vers closed her eyes briefly, felt the buzzing start at the back of her head, and let the power build.

CHAPTER 12

The buzzing in her ears. It was all Vers could hear at that moment. She opened her eyes and looked around, and saw only chaos. There had to be hundreds of vines now, swirling, swinging, stabbing at the three occupants of the tunnel.

The hair on the back of her neck stood on end. Vers felt the power flowing into her hands, gathering in her fingertips.

The vines had encircled Minn-Erva. Despite her attempts to shoot and fight her way free, the vines were winning. Minn-Erva screamed as one of the vines struck at her, through the armor on her chest.

Vers couldn't even see the Skrull now; his body had been completely entangled in vines.

The buzzing grew louder, and louder still, until Vers could no longer hold anything back.

Pure, blinding photon energy streamed from her hands and into the membrane in front of her. Almost instantly, the membrane exploded into a million tiny pieces, spraying Vers, Minn-Erva, and the Skrull in the process and covering them with flecks of the filmy material.

Vers wiped the specks of goo out of her eyes. She had done it.

But in doing so, she had also unleashed a torrent of mud from the cavern that now flowed freely into the tunnel. The sudden force of it knocked her back, and she slammed into the wall. The vines lashed out, trying to grab her, but Vers managed to pull herself free. She barely had time to take one last breath of oxygen before the tunnel became completely flooded.

Then she turned to Minn-Erva, who was now almost entirely enveloped, just like the Skrull. Vers pointed her fists at the wall right behind her, where the vines were snaking from, and unleashed another burst of photon energy.

The vines sizzled as they were sliced in half, burnt off at the point where Vers's blast had struck them. The half that had captured Minn-Erva immediately went slack, lifeless, and Minn-Erva fell to the ground.

Vers swiveled to face the vines that had trapped the Skrull. She managed another burst, destroying the vines behind him. They, too, dropped away, leaving the Skrull to slump down into the muck and mud.

Though Minn-Erva was now free, she seemed to be struggling from her fight with the vines and the sudden lack of oxygen. Vers grabbed her by the arm. She swam over to the Skrull, who appeared to be unconscious. She took him by the waist and pulled him close.

Then she headed for the broken membrane

and swam through, tugging Minn-Erva and the Skrull along with her.

"I'm fine, I'm fine," Minn-Erva panted, but even as the warrior protested Vers's efforts, she clung to Vers, her body confirming a weakened state that her pride wouldn't let her admit to.

Vers rolled her eyes. *Stubborn to the last,* she thought. "Minn-Erva, don't waste your energy on resisting me," she said. "Let me help."

Minn-Erva fell silent, but Vers felt her tighten her hold marginally, which she took as a sign of assent. She trudged on.

Inside, the cavern was a vast sea of translucent muck. As Vers stared up toward the surface, she saw that the Kree fighter was still there.

So far, so good, she thought.

On her own, the trip from the cavern toward the surface would have been a struggle. The muck didn't allow for any kind of rapid movement. It resisted each stroke, tried to push her back even as she was trying to pull ahead.

Add two passengers to the effort, and it was nearly impossible.

But Vers wasn't giving up. She wasn't ready to die. Not today.

Not ever.

With all her might, she kicked upward over and over, driving herself and her two companions slowly, inexorably toward the surface.

Down below, she could see that the cavern was ringed with membranes, just like the one Vers had just emerged through. One by one, the membranes were now opening, and vines began to snake out.

Hundreds.

Thousands.

They were slowly slithering through the muck, winding their way toward Vers.

It seemed whatever this thing was really wanted to keep them right where they were. If the planet really were like a cancer, then the vines must be trying to absorb her. To feed off of them for fuel to keep surviving.

Gross.

She was near the surface now, and only a few meters away from the ship. Yet it seemed so far. The vines were snaking closer and closer, and the muck seemed to be getting thicker toward the surface. It was becoming increasingly difficult for Vers to make any progress whatsoever.

Realizing that she couldn't go any farther in her current state, Vers decided to lighten her load. She let go of the Skrull briefly, and he stayed still, suspended in the surrounding muck, like a fly in amber. Then she grabbed hold of Minn-Erva's waist. Summoning all her strength, Vers pushed Minn-Erva forward, up to the surface and toward the ship.

Vers watched as she saw Minn-Erva slowly ascend until her body broke through the muck. She wasn't sure if Minn-Erva was even still conscious at this point.

Then it was the Skrull's turn. She reached out for the unconscious alien, grabbed him around his waist, and shoved him toward the surface as well.

Now it was her turn. She kicked hard.

Nothing happened.

The muck above her seemed to be pushing her down, farther and farther. The more she kicked and fought, the more she struggled, the more the muck seemed to press back.

Vers couldn't comprehend what was happening. All she knew was that she couldn't hold her breath any longer, and the surface wasn't any closer.

But the vines were.

They had already grabbed her left leg, and Vers could feel their force pulling her down below.

Thinking that she might have enough in her for one last photon blast, Vers pointed a fist at the vine. The buzzing sound slowly filled her ears, when it was abruptly overpowered by a high-pitched whining sound.

Vers jerked as she saw a sliver of light pierce through the muck, hitting the vine, severing it in two.

Minn-Erva.

Vers kicked as hard as she could, and pointed both hands toward the surface. The buzzing in her head built up once more, as the hairs on the back of her neck pricked up.

With one last-ditch effort, she blasted through the muck above.

CHAPTER 13

"You in any kind of shape to fly this thing?" Minn-Erva yelled in Vers's direction. Apparently recovered from her bout with the vines, Minn-Erva was standing on the hull of the Kree fighter, firing her blaster repeatedly into the muck below. Vines were breaking the surface by the dozen, all of them desperately grabbing for the ship, and the three life-forms that stood atop it.

Vers was trying to catch her breath, clutching the side of the ship. She had barely managed to escape from the muck, even with Minn-Erva's intervention and her own abilities. In the process, she had expended an incredible amount of photon energy, and felt like she was in a daze.

But if Minn-Erva could push through, so could she. "I can fly anything, anywhere," Vers said, and she meant it. A vine whipped past her face, but she didn't even flinch. She opened the fighter hatch, then grabbed the unconscious but still-breathing Skrull, and shoved him inside.

Minn-Erva kept on blasting away, keeping the vines subdued. Every now and then, one would slip through, but Vers managed to neutralize them before they took hold.

She slipped into the hatch and hopped into the pilot's seat. She switched on the engines, avoiding any and all pre-flight procedures that were required to warm up the ship. There wasn't any time for that.

"If you wanna come with, you better get in here now!" Vers hollered, hoping that she was loud enough to be heard outside.

A second later, she heard a clang as the hatch

shut tight. Minn-Erva was standing inside the ship, clutching her left arm. She was bleeding.

"Get this bucket out of here," she said with a grimace.

"With pleasure," Vers replied, and she yanked back on the ship's yoke as the thrusters fired at maximum strength.

The craft exploded from the surface, blasting a crater into the muck. The air was filled with the most piercing sound Vers had ever heard. She wanted desperately to cover her ears with her hands, but she couldn't—it took everything she had to keep both hands on the yoke.

The sound cut through the hull of the ship itself. Minn-Erva made her way to the copilot's seat and strapped herself in. "What is that sound?" Minn-Erva asked, as it started to fade the farther they got from the surface.

"The planet was screaming," Vers said.

Within seconds, the ship had punched through the atmosphere of what had once been

Aphos Prime, again moving with such blinding speed as to avoid detection by any Skrull sensors.

Both warriors visibly relaxed as the decimated, diseased shell of a planet receded farther and farther in the distance. Vers cast a glance over her shoulder at the Skrull, who was still passed out, his chest rising and falling weakly. She turned back toward Minn-Erva.

"Thanks," Vers said. "For what you did back there."

"You would have done the same for me," Minn-Erva said, not looking at Vers. "And, in fact, you kind of did. So thank you for that."

Vers barely suppressed a laugh.

"What's so funny?" Minn-Erva asked.

"I told you that you'd thank me before the mission was over," Vers said with a grin. "Look who was right!"

CHAPTER 14

"What about the Skrull prisoner?" Vers asked.

"He will be interrogated. Then we will decide what to do with him," Yon-Rogg said. The pair walked along the hallway toward the briefing chamber. The other members of Starforce—Minn-Erva, Att-Lass, Bron-Char, and Korath—were waiting for them.

Vers couldn't resist asking the question that had been troubling her since the realization on Aphos Prime of what the planet truly was, and what very real danger she and Minn-Erva had been placed into by the Kree. "Yon-Rogg . . . did you know about Aphos Prime?"

Vers asked. "And, if you did—why didn't you warn us?"

"We had no idea," Yon-Rogg said. "What happened on Aphos Prime is a mystery to us all." He waved his hand, as though declaring the topic closed to further discussion. "Now prepare for the briefing."

Vers was frustrated as she walked ahead of her commander toward the briefing room. She felt that Yon-Rogg knew more, that there was something he wasn't telling her.

Despite the peril they'd faced, the mission to Aphos Prime had been an important one. Vers and Minn-Erva had uncovered a terrible power, and at least they'd brought back a witness who could potentially provide more information. And, Vers had to admit, she'd learned that she could get along with Minn-Erva well enough to complete a mission. They'd even had each other's backs, which shouldn't have surprised her, but it did.

As Vers approached the door to the briefing

chamber, she looked behind her, and saw Yon-Rogg type something into his tablet.

If she had been able to see the screen, Vers would have seen the words *Aphos Prime/Peer Kaal/ test complete.*

But she would have to wait to learn what they meant.

BUT THAT WAS THEN.
THIS IS . . .

NOW

CHAPTER 15

"Leave her!"

"We're not leaving." *SSSHHRRRZZZZZKKKK.* "—not an option."

KRRRZZZZZZZKKK. "—compromised every-thing!"

ZRRRKKKKKKKK. "—don't trust—" *KRRRRRKKK.*

The chatter over her comm-link cut in and out, the static obscuring most of the words, squawking in her ears, nearly deafening. But Vers had heard enough.

She was in trouble.

Not that she needed to hear any of the comm-link back-and-forth to know it. For starters, there was the six-inch-long gash in her right leg. Then there was the blue blood that flowed freely from the wound—which stubbornly refused to close, thanks to the Xandarian knife that she had unceremoniously yanked from her leg less than a minute ago.

Then there was the twisted body of the Xandarian scientist who lay before her, lifeless. Peer Kaal.

It hadn't happened by her hand. No, that had been a direct result of the explosion. The one that had destroyed the bunker that Vers had so stealthily invaded. It was a miracle she was still alive.

Peer hadn't been quite as lucky.

Vers gasped in pain, trying to draw in a breath of fresh air. Her lungs burned, and her pulse thrummed in her temples, matching the ceaseless throb in her leg. With every beat, a little more blood pumped through the wound, forming a small pool on the concrete floor beneath her.

She winced, blinking a few times to clear her eyes. They were blurry, and she rubbed them. Light-headedness overtook her as her temples began to ache more insistently.

Pull it together, Vers. No one's gonna get you out of this. You're on your own.

So get a grip.

And get a good look.

Sitting up, craning her neck, she scanned from left to right, taking in her situation. Trapped in a bombed-out bunker, crouched behind a pile of rubble. Xandarians on the ridge to her left, and down the passageway to the right. How many were there? She couldn't tell; they were too well-hidden. Were they Nova Corps? The one who tried to kill her mere moments before certainly wasn't. The Nova Corps operated under at least some code of conduct, of honor—Vers knew this. They didn't typically carry knives and go the route of assassins, sneaking up behind their prey.

Unless she was wrong about the Xandarians, and Yon-Rogg was right.

Yon-Rogg is always right.

Unless . . . this time he isn't.

Vers slid along the ground, pulling her wounded leg through the debris, leaving a trail of blood in her wake. She tore a piece of fabric from the pant of her uniform and tied it around the gash. The makeshift tourniquet seemed to stanch the bleeding a little—but only a little.

If she didn't get out of there, and soon, she would bleed out.

She needed to rejoin her teammates.

If they hadn't already left her for dead.

I screwed up, I screwed up, I screwed up. . . .

CHAPTER 16

It seemed like just yesterday that Vers had, as usual, been trying to outpace her demons on her morning run. Her feet hit the ground, pounding one after the other. The pace was relentless. She had to keep running.

Stay focused.

And she did stay focused. So focused that she didn't even see it coming. At the last second, when she finally became aware, it was already too late.

"Hey!"

The old man went barreling over onto the pavement as Vers collided with his side. He slammed into the hard surface, landing with a resounding *thump* and rubbing his tailbone as he glared up at her. Her own momentum nearly threw her to the ground as well, but she caught herself, hopping on first her right then her left foot, maintaining her balance before coming to a stop.

"Why don't you watch where you're going? I oughtta—"

The man, balding, with sparse hair around his temples, furrowed his brow as he looked up at Vers. She saw the expression on his face, the confusion and apprehension, as he took in the pale skin and fair hair that marked her as "different." That look changed as his eyes glanced quickly at the clothes she wore and the insignia displayed upon them. Suddenly, his surly demeanor changed. "I'm sorry," he said, his tone suddenly soft and placating. "So, so sorry; all my fault."

Vers extended a hand. "No, it was my fault," she said. Her breathing was calm and controlled, even though she had been out running for nearly an hour. "I should have watched where I was going, but—"

The man waved Vers's hand away. "No, please, I should have been more aware of my surroundings. Thank you for your service," he said, as he pulled himself to his feet and dusted off his knees, wincing a bit, but turning his grimace into a smile when he noticed Vers was still watching him closely.

"Are you sure you're okay?"

"Perfectly fine," he said, scurrying away with an odd little bow.

Vers scratched the back of her head, then put both hands on her hips, bending over slightly. She took in a deep breath. She still wasn't used to the automatic deference that came with being a member of Starforce. As a member of the Kree's most elite combat team, Vers, along with her teammates, had been charged with defending the people and property of the Kree Empire. It was a mission that she took quite seriously, and it was an undertaking that was honored and respected by the citizens of the Kree Empire as well.

She watched for a moment as the man

faded into the early-morning distance, then started her run again. The other members of Starforce often commented on her training regimen, especially Minn-Erva.

Why do you run outside? Minn-Erva had asked more than once, the scorn obvious in her tone. *It is a pointless activity. There are so many better ways to prepare for battle.*

Why did she run? It helped clear her head, for one thing. When she ran, Vers could erase her mind of everything, even that nagging thought that tugged at the back of her mind. Like a memory that was just out of reach, something that she could never bring into view. A lingering refrain, occupying space but remaining stubbornly elusive.

Her feet hit the ground, and soon Vers had established her rhythm once more. White noise filled her ears, as the sounds of her breathing and her heartbeat drowned out the external sounds of the city. She was an early riser these days, though she had the sense that she had always been one to wake early. She couldn't remember. That bothered her.

Vers looked up at the tall buildings that rose up toward the sky. Everything had an angular look to it—sharp and abrupt. There were a few curves in the architecture, and Vers found that interesting. The buildings seemed to match the personality of Hala's people, she thought.

Keep running.

Run so you don't have to think.

Thinking is what gets a person in my line of work killed.

CHAPTER 17

Yon-Rogg was a man of action, not words. The more action and the fewer words, the better.

The briefing had been mercifully short. The mission clear and concisely relayed, albeit difficult to swallow. But as the leader and commander of the most elite Kree fighting unit, Yon-Rogg was accustomed to difficult. He was used to near-impossible. He had definitely been through worse.

Still, it was only part one. There would be another briefing later that day, this time with the entire Starforce assembled. Yon-Rogg shook his head, and ran a hand through his bristly short hair.

They'll be ready, he had told his superiors.

Starforce was always ready. And he believed in them. Every single one.

But he knew that there were certain members of his crew who didn't necessarily feel the same.

If Starforce was going to pull off this mission, Yon-Rogg would need everyone working together, cooperating, watching each other's back.

He couldn't afford even one slipup.

And that meant he had to keep an eye on Vers.

"Wow, you're outside already," Vers commented. "Usually I'm the one who has to ring your doorbell."

Yon-Rogg stood outside his apartment, wearing his workout clothes, as Vers jogged up alongside him.

"I'm always ready," he said. "Even when I'm not."

The two started down the street. "Also, I

admire your enthusiasm and drive," Yon-Rogg said.

"Is that code for 'Please stop showing up at my home at the crack of dawn'?" Vers asked with a grin.

"Basically," Yon-Rogg replied. He wasn't joking.

Vers shrugged as they ran in perfect lock-step down the quiet, mostly empty street. There was little activity in the city this time of morning. A few people heading home from their jobs on the night shift, and a few heading to work early.

"I ran into somebody on the way over to your place," Vers said, making conversation, her words evenly punctuated and her breaths coming easy despite their accelerated pace.

"Anyone I know?" he asked.

"No, I mean I literally *ran* into somebody. Just plowed right into them," Vers said, illustrating her point by slamming her right hand into her left.

"You and your running," Yon-Rogg said,

shaking his head. "You're insatiable. I don't understand it."

"Maybe if you tried it, you would."

Yon-Rogg looked at Vers and smiled. Their runs to the gym were more than sufficient for him. Running was useful to Yon-Rogg only as a necessary means to a desired end; to Vers, it appeared an end in and of itself. "I will let you have all the fun," he said.

The gym was empty when they arrived. It was nothing fancy, just an old place, but it suited the two warriors' purposes just fine. Yon-Rogg motioned for Vers to join him on the mat, then raised his hands. He looked at his opponent and nodded.

She's unfocused, I can tell.

We can't afford that.

"Are you ready?" Yon-Rogg asked, his right hand beckoning toward Vers.

"Question is, are *you* ready?" came her answer. She set herself in attack position, and threw a roundhouse kick with her right leg. Yon-Rogg sidestepped it, ducking. Then he grabbed her leg with his left hand, and slammed his right hand into her calf.

Vers grunted as she nearly hit the mat. She caught herself, landing on her left knee. Her hands hit the mat, and she went into a roll, coming to a rest on her feet.

"Good," Yon-Rogg said. "If you're going to come at me with such a clumsy attack, at least know how to roll out of it."

"Who says that was an attack? I'm just probing for signs of weakness," Vers said, a confident smile on her face.

"A little less joking, a little more fighting," Yon-Rogg said. Then he thrust out his right arm as Vers ducked down to her right, Yon-Rogg's hand just missing her neck. Still in a crouched position, Vers kicked out her left leg, sweeping Yon-Rogg's legs from beneath him so he landed on his back. He hit the mat with a dull thud.

Yon-Rogg blinked. When he opened his eyes, he saw Vers kneeling over him, right hand raised just inches from his eyes, ready to strike.

"Think I found that weakness," Vers said, still smiling.

She takes this too lightly.

She needs to learn that you can never drop your guard.

Without a word, Yon-Rogg's right hand flashed out, knocking away Vers's hand, throwing her off-balance.

Never.

A second later, Yon-Rogg was back on his feet. Caught off guard, Vers staggered backward, allowing him to land blow after blow to her midsection. They weren't killing blows— just enough force to knock the wind out of one's opponent, and make breathing nearly impossible.

Now it was Vers's turn to eat mat.

Vers gasped, trying to force her reluctant lungs to take in some much-needed air.

"That lesson was a long time coming," Yon-Rogg said, standing over her.

Slowly, the pain subsided, and Vers was finally able to catch her breath. "I suppose you think you won," she gritted out through staggered inhales, struggling into a sitting position.

"If you don't learn how to take this seriously, you're going to end up dead," Yon-Rogg said. His voice maintained its even keel; he wasn't being dramatic, it was just a simple statement of fact.

"I know this is hard for you to believe, but I do take this seriously," Vers said, somewhat defensive. "The training, the mission, Starforce . . . all of it."

"I know you think you do," said Yon-Rogg. "And I know that you have potential."

"Why do I sense a *but* coming?" Vers asked.

Yon-Rogg turned his back as Vers got up from the mat. They walked to the edge. Yon-Rogg then grabbed a towel from the floor, and threw it to Vers. He grabbed his own towel and proceeded to dry the sweat from his face.

"You can't have any doubts," Yon-Rogg said.

"*I* know you are good enough to be a part of this team. But *you* need to know it."

He pointed an outstretched index finger at Vers's head. "I can't pretend to know what goes on in there," Yon-Rogg began, "but if you can't keep your head clear and stay focused . . ."

Vers let out a loud sigh, running the towel across her face. "I am a Kree warrior," she said. "Don't doubt me."

Then she threw the towel in Yon-Rogg's face. The next thing he knew, he felt a foot in his gut and a sharp blow to the base of his neck. Yon-Rogg spluttered, tossing the towel to the side as he jumped back into attack mode.

Don't give me a reason to.

CHAPTER 18

A sharp stab of pain jolted Vers back to her present.

No matter how bad things get, they can always get worse. A lot worse.

It was supposed to be a simple mission. Get in, get out. Not bleed out.

The Kree had been bleeding for years. Bleeding in a seemingly endless war with the Xandarians. Bleeding manpower. Bleeding resources.

There had been too much blood.

This mission was supposed to change all that. It would turn the tide, tip the balance of power in favor of the Kree. *Peace was coming,* they said. Negotiations were rumored to be taking place at the highest levels. But there were those among the Kree military who believed that peace could only come through strength.

Starforce was their strength.

Vers gasped audibly as she grabbed her leg. The makeshift tourniquet was just barely doing its job. Her leg throbbed, and she felt the warm, sticky blood saturating the bandage, as small trails of blue trickled down past her calf.

Not good. At least no one's actively shooting at me right now.

Peering through a crack in the broken foundation, she looked into the distance where she had previously noted her Xandarian opponents. There was no sign of them, no indication of movement. Seizing the opportunity, Vers attempted to stand up, to escape her pinned-down position to a safer locale where she could at least hope for extraction, or rescue by her team.

She tried to balance on the leg, but it gave out almost instantly, unable to take her weight.

However bad she had thought the leg injury was, it was obviously even worse.

A *lot* worse.

Vers bit her lip, drawing in a deep breath. She held it, then let it out.

Focus. Stay focused. Push past the pain.

Again, she attempted to stand. This time, she made it. The pain was blinding. But the leg didn't buckle, and neither did she. Vers had no idea how long the leg would hold out before it would be completely useless. She leaned against the foundation, moving along as quickly as she could, her wounded leg dragging behind her. With her right hand, she wiped away the blood that was running down her leg.

Don't leave a trail for anyone to follow.

She was now at the edge of the foundation, and Vers wobbled, suddenly light-headed. She was dizzy, unable to get her bearings.

Not good, not good.

"I think I saw movement!"

The voice came out of nowhere and brought Vers back into the moment.

Stay focused. . . .

She threw her back against the foundation, ceasing all motion, and held her breath. She waited for someone to respond to the first voice, but she heard only quiet. Then Vers could make out the sound of feet crunching along the rubble. They were close, but not on top of her position. Not yet.

Think there's only one of them.

Slowly, Vers turned her neck, so she was barely able to look beyond the stone outcropping. And she saw him. The uniform was a dead giveaway.

Definitely Nova.

The Nova Corps officer looked to be about six feet tall, muscular, a little beefy. He brandished a wrist-mounted blaster on his right hand, and Vers noticed that his finger was gently tapping it, like a nervous tic. The officer was looking around, eyes moving left-right, left-right.

Trying to draw a bead on me.

She wondered where the other Nova were.

They should have called out by now. Unless something had happened to them?

Or someone?

Vers sat stock-still, planning her next move. It was either wait it out and hope the Nova didn't find her, or take him down quickly. There was no way she could sneak out of there without him noticing, not now. Her mind raced through her training, all those early-morning combat sessions with Yon-Rogg. She knew dozens of ways to incapacitate a foe with her bare hands. Some of them nonlethal. But with her bum leg, she would need to figure out a way to make her move while standing still.

Leaning against the stone, she looked around the corner again. The Nova wasn't there, but she could still hear the sound of feet coming closer.

Closer still.

For a moment, Vers forgot about her leg, until she tried to take a deep breath and instead felt a stinging sensation running the length of her windpipe. Her throat felt tight and ached when she tried to swallow. The light-headed feeling was still there, too.

The sound of shifting stones.

Closer.

Stay focused.

This hurts, this hurts, this hurts, this hurts. . . .

Closer.

Then her hand suddenly shot out, and squeezed.

CHAPTER 19

Before they'd been sent out on the mission that day, Minn-Erva had been spending the day much like any other as Starforce's best sniper: practicing her shot. She hefted the rifle in her hands, feeling its satisfying weight in her grasp. Then she placed the rifle's stock firmly against her right shoulder and peered through the scope. The target was only about three hundred meters ahead. She was used to banking shots like these in her sleep. But that was the point of all this training, wasn't it?

She pulled the trigger and squeezed off one round.

Then another.

And another.

"Excellent shooting," came a disembodied, hollow-sounding voice. "Shots fired: three. Direct hits: three. Damage assessment: maximum fatality."

"'Maximum Fatality' should be the name of your band."

Minn-Erva rolled her eyes. She didn't even bother to look at Att-Lass as he spoke. She could hear the snap of him loading a pistol as he walked up behind her.

"You're just like *her*," Minn-Erva said, raising the rifle to her shoulder once more and taking aim at the target. "You think this is all a joke."

"Yon-Rogg has faith in her," Att-Lass said, taking his spot in the firing range. "I have faith in her."

"Is faith gonna help you when you're pinned down in a firefight and you need someone to drop the enemy before you're dead?" Minn-Erva said hotly, firing off another series of shots. Each one a direct hit. Just like before, the shots would have proven fatal had they hit a living being.

"Excellent shooting," said Att-Lass, in perfect time with the electronic voice over the speaker. "Shots fired: two. Direct hits: two. Damage assessment: maximum fatality."

"Keep talking, and *you're* going to experience 'maximum fatality,'" Minn-Erva snapped.

"Duly noted," Att-Lass replied.

An hour later, Minn-Erva walked away from the firing range and checked her weapons into a storage locker. Att-Lass followed behind, checking in his twin pistols.

"Why do you ride her so hard?" Att-Lass asked.

"You know damn well why," Minn-Erva shot back.

"What, because she's Yon-Rogg's favorite?"

"Yon-Rogg doesn't play favorites," Minn-Erva

said, wincing at how false that statement sounded even to her own ears. She opened the door to the narrow hallway, walking down the dimly lit tunnel that led to a lone yellow door at the end. When she reached the door, it slid open and she stepped inside, Att-Lass right behind her. "Ground level," she said, and the elevator rapidly descended from the sixty-eighth floor of the building.

"Before Vers showed up, you were the golden child," Att-Lass said. "Now that she's here . . ." His voice trailed off, but she knew what he was suggesting.

"We're Starforce," Minn-Erva said flatly. "We're here to do a job. A job that no one else wants to do. That no one else *can* do. I'd put my life on the line for any of you. I just want to know that she'll do the same, when the time comes."

"She'll pull her weight," Att-Lass said. The elevator door opened, revealing the busy street beyond.

A typical day on Hala.

As the duo stepped out onto the street, the passersby took notice of their uniforms and immediately cut them a wide berth.

They're counting on us to save them. All of them.

"She'd better," Minn-Erva said over her shoulder as she broke away from Att-Lass and walked off alone.

CHAPTER 20

The chamber was small and poorly lit, and the ventilation was awful. The situation wasn't helped by the massive presence of Bron-Char. The man was built like a wall—even bigger and sturdier, maybe—and he alone seemed to take up half the dark blue quarters. The ceiling was low, and he had to crouch just to fit. He stood there, impassive, stroking his beard with his right hand.

"What do you make of all this?" Vers asked, pacing along the luminescent floor.

"I think," Bron-Char said, slowly, "that you need to stop walking back and forth. I'm getting dizzy just watching you."

Vers didn't react, and she certainly didn't stop pacing. "I just saw Yon-Rogg this morning, and he didn't mention anything," she said. "Something strange is going on."

"Perhaps," Bron-Char agreed, his back to one of the room's featureless walls. "Strange can be good. It keeps things interesting."

"You remember the last time things got 'interesting'?" Vers asked.

The straight line that was Bron-Char's mouth slowly turned upward into what appeared to be a slight smile. "Of course I do," Bron-Char said. "But who knew it was going to bite?"

"Well, I did. Minn-Erva did. Att-Lass— Come to think of it, we *all* knew that the creature would bite."

The smile on Bron-Char's face grew a little larger, until it could almost be described as a grin. "You like being right, don't you?"

"I like being alive," Vers retorted.

"Let's stay that way," Yon-Rogg said as he entered through the door to the chamber. He didn't appear hurried, but his demeanor was all business. At his side stood a tall man who appeared equally serious, maybe even more so. The second man greeted Bron-Char and Vers with identically sharp nods, punctual and exact, the way he did everything.

"Yon-Rogg," Vers said, addressing the leader of Starforce. "Korath," she added, recognizing the team's second-in-command.

The door closed behind the two men. Yon-Rogg set a small tablet down on the table in the middle of the chamber. Without looking up, he said, "Where are Att-Lass and Minn-Erva?"

As if on cue, the door slid open and in walked Minn-Erva, followed a few seconds later by Att-Lass. The entire Starforce team had now been assembled.

"What's the situation?" Minn-Erva said, her voice all business, but a bit edgier than usual. She looked at Vers, then at Yon-Rogg.

Yon-Rogg didn't react one way or another to Minn-Erva's tone. Swiftly, he pressed an index finger to the surface of the tablet. In the air directly above, a holographic diagram of the Kree sector of space appeared. Planets occupied or under Kree control were cast in a blue hue. "The Kree are at war. This is not news. We have been at war since before any of us were born. Since before any of our parents were born." Yon-Rogg looked at Vers, and she met his eyes, then felt color come to her face and averted her gaze. She didn't even know who her parents were, let alone where they were born.

With a swipe of his index finger, Yon-Rogg shifted the holographic diagram, until the planets it showed were now a luminescent green.

"The war against the Skrulls is ongoing," Yon-Rogg said, gesturing to those green planets. "More and more, the shape-shifters are occupying planets in the outer territories. They are merciless. As a result, we're forced to marshal more soldiers, more weapons . . .

more, more, more. It is a drain on the not-unlimited resources of the Kree Empire."

"So, let me guess," Vers chimed in. "We're gonna hold a bake sale?"

"What is a bake sale?" Korath asked, in all seriousness.

"I, too, would like to know what this 'bake sale' is," Bron-Char added.

Yon-Rogg continued, as if no one had said anything. "In order to divert all men and materials to the Skrull war effort, the Supreme Intelligence informs me that there is talk of ending our ongoing conflicts with others in the interest of conserving and diverting resources."

"'Others'?" Minn-Erva echoed. "But you can't mean . . . Xandar?"

"That's impossible," Att-Lass said in disbelief.

Uncharacteristically, Vers was silent. Instead, she just sat back in her chair, waiting for the room to quiet down and for Yon-Rogg to resume speaking. "The conflict against Xandar draws vital resources away from our fight with the Skrulls," he said, almost as if trying to convince himself. "Therefore, yes, the prospect of a peace treaty with Xandar has been broached."

The room fell silent. The Kree had been at war with the planet Xandar and its inhabitants for centuries, with neither side being able to gain enough of an upper hand to end the conflict. The Kree military had invested endless warriors and resources to gain an edge—and now, with a peace of necessity on the horizon, it would all have been for nothing.

"What's our mission?" Vers asked into the heavy quiet that had settled over the room.

Yon-Rogg swiped the tablet again, bringing an orange-colored world into view.

"Starforce has been ordered to infiltrate Sy'gyl, where we are to make contact with a possible Xandarian defector. We are to obtain plans for a weapon being developed by the

Xandarians, and bring both the defector and the plans back with us," Yon-Rogg explained.

"Sy'gyl is deep in Xandarian space," Minn-Erva said. "That's occupied territory. We'll be on our own."

"You like being on your own," Yon-Rogg replied. Minn-Erva smiled.

"If we're so close to peace, why jeopardize it with this mission?" Vers asked. Minn-Erva glared at her like she had asked the most obvious, most ridiculous question.

Korath eyed Vers. "If peace does come to pass between our worlds, we must ensure that the Kree remain in a position of power," he said, matter-of-factly.

Yon-Rogg nodded. "Having the Xandarian weapon puts us in that position," he added. "The Kree can never be subservient to Xandar."

Vers nodded, unconvinced. Couldn't Starforce be put to better use elsewhere, such as against the Skrulls, if the whole point of ending the

Xandarian war was to focus on their shape-changing enemies? There was something about the mission that was unsettling, and Vers couldn't put her finger on it.

"We leave within the hour. Meet at the hangar at eleven hundred hours," Yon-Rogg said, picking up the tablet and exiting the chamber. Korath looked at everyone, and with a final nod, followed suit.

CHAPTER 21

"What's bothering you?"

Minn-Erva looked at Vers as the meeting broke up.

"Why should anything be bothering me?" Vers replied. She stood up, shoved her seat against the table, and moved toward the door, walking past Minn-Erva. Vers had long sensed the fierce warrior's dislike of her, and over time the feeling had become quite mutual.

"Just seems like something is. Not that I care," Minn-Erva said, practically waving her hand as if to dismiss Vers's question.

Vers turned around and glared at Minn-Erva. "Then why ask?"

Minn-Erva gazed up for a second, then bit

her bottom lip. Then she stared directly into Vers's eyes and said bluntly, "I'm just wondering when you're going to slip up."

So that's what this is all about.

"Keep waiting," Vers threw over her shoulder, continuing toward the door. "It ain't gonna happen."

"Vers is one of us now," Att-Lass chimed in. "She's just as much a part of Starforce as you or me or Bron-Char."

Bron-Char nodded in agreement, his bulky head bobbing up and down.

"Yes, she's one of us," Minn-Erva said. "She better remember that when it comes time to make difficult choices."

What the hell is that supposed to mean?

Vers felt her temper start to flare, then remembered what Yon-Rogg had been telling her during their training sessions.

Stay focused.

Getting into it with Minn-Erva wouldn't help her or the dynamic of the team, especially as they were about to head into a new and potentially dangerous mission.

"You certainly have a way with people," Vers heard Bron-Char remark to Minn-Erva as the doors slid shut behind her.

Vers marched down the hallway, turning Minn-Erva's cryptic words over in her mind. It was true she hadn't been a member of Starforce all that long. Certainly not as long as the others. But Vers pulled her weight, and she knew it. So why did Minn-Erva always have to try to knock her down a peg? Why did she always make it out that Vers was a "weak link" who wouldn't come through in the clutch?

Girl's got a chip on her shoulder big as Bron-Char.

Vers shook off her annoyance about Minn-Erva and turned her thoughts instead to the upcoming mission. There was still something about it that wasn't sitting right with her. She knew that the Xandarian conflict

had been the all-consuming problem fac-
ing the Kree for centuries. But ever since the
Skrull War started, it had become clear that
the Xandarians were the proverbial lesser of
two evils.

Is the enemy of my enemy my friend?

The prospect of a lasting peace between
the Kree and Xandar would have monumen-
tal implications for the Kree effort against the
Skrulls, no doubt. But something about the
plan to gain the upper hand against Xandar in
the eleventh hour, right before a peace treaty
might be signed, made Vers feel uneasy. For
all she had learned of Xandar, its inhabitants
had always seemed to be an honorable people.
True, they lacked the warrior spirit that the
Kree possessed, the rigorous conviction that
they were always right.

Maybe that's a good thing.

Vers reached the end of the hallway, when
she heard a voice calling after her.

"Don't let Minn-Erva get to you."

Att-Lass.

"She didn't get to me at all." Vers sighed, turning to face her fellow warrior. "I'm used to it. Aren't we all used to it by now?"

Att-Lass smiled. "You know how it is. You're the newest recruit to the team. It takes Minn-Erva a while before she trusts anyone. I mean, look at me. She didn't trust me until—"

"She still doesn't trust you," Vers cut in as a yellow door slid open in front of her. She stepped in, and Att-Lass followed.

"Maybe she doesn't trust anyone except Yon-Rogg," Att-Lass admitted. "Before you came along . . ."

"Yeah, I know—she was the teacher's pet."

Att-Lass stared at Vers as the yellow door slid shut, and the elevator began to move down. "Okay, I don't know what that is, but I'll assume it's something not nice."

How does he not know what a "teacher's pet" is? Doesn't everyone know what that means? We all say that around here—don't we?

Vers laughed. "It just means that she was Yon-Rogg's favorite."

There was a glint of recognition and understanding in Att-Lass's eyes. "Yes, well, that's certainly true. But I think Yon-Rogg realizes what a valuable addition your . . . skills are to the team, and that the extra training required to utilize those skills correctly is entirely worthwhile."

"You've thought about this, haven't you?"

"I care about the people on my team," Att-Lass reasoned.

The elevator reached the bottom floor, and the yellow door slid open. Vers nodded and walked out, Att-Lass right behind her.

✻

Vers arrived at the hangar in her combat uniform. It was designed to accommodate a wide range of motion, as well as her particular . . . abilities. She was greeted by an unusual sight. Instead of the *Helion*, the ship that usually carried Starforce on their missions, there was a battered freighter with Xandarian markings.

"Don't tell me this is our ride," Vers remarked before she could stop herself.

I just said that out loud, didn't I?

Yon-Rogg turned toward her from where he was overseeing the transfer of munitions into the freighter's cargo bay. "Is there something wrong with it?"

Vers shook her head. "No. I'm just not used to traveling incognito. And I'm not used to the subterfuge, either."

"We can't afford to be recognized," Yon-Rogg said as the other members of Starforce assembled, all in their full fighter uniforms. "We're heading deep into Xandarian space. If we're flagged, the mission is over before it starts. At least this way we have a chance."

Nodding her head, Vers watched as she saw a woman she didn't recognize enter the cockpit. She was short, with close-cropped black hair. "Who's that?"

"Pilot," Minn-Erva answered. "Someone who knows the territory."

"Xandarian?" Vers asked.

"You mean does she know Xandarian territory, or is she Xandarian?" Att-Lass said.

"Both, I guess," Vers replied.

"She's Kree," Korath said, staring straight
into Vers's eyes. Then he looked at Minn-Erva
and Att-Lass, with the same super-serious,
utterly humorless expression. "That is Sun-Val,
and she has our complete trust. You will treat
her as one of Starforce."

"Sir, yes, sir," Vers said, offering a salute.

Korath tilted his head slightly, looking at
Vers. "You confuse me."

CHAPTER 22

"You're . . . hurting . . . me. . . ."

Back on Sy'gyl, Vers's hand was wrapped so tightly around her would-be assailant's throat, she was surprised he hadn't already passed out. She was cutting off the supply of oxygen, practically crushing his windpipe. How he was able to even force words out was a mystery.

There's a lotta fight in this guy.

She pulled her arm inward, bringing the man in a Nova Corps uniform into full view. He struggled against Vers's grip, his curly brown hair thrashing wildly with the rest of him.

"You're . . . bleeding," he managed to get out, his voice sounding like sandpaper.

"You will be, too, if you don't shut up," Vers said, squeezing a little harder. The man gasped as she did so.

"I'm not here . . . to . . . hurt you," he managed to say.

"You're in no position to hurt anybody," Vers replied. "Ever again."

"I can . . . get you out of . . . here . . . alive."

What is he talking about?

"Weren't you just firing at me?" Vers asked.

The man shook his head no—at least, as much as he was able to with Vers's hand at his throat.

I'm about to do something really dumb.

Vers released her grip, and the man crumpled to the ground. He clutched at his throat with both hands, gasping for air.

"You're . . . strong," he choked out at long last.

"Name and rank," Vers shot back, ignoring the man's statement entirely.

"Rhomann Dey, Nova Corps. Rank"—he let out a hacking cough—"Corpsman," he finished. "I'm here to help you."

"You're here to do what, now?" Vers said incredulously. "Aren't we at war or something?"

Dey nodded while rubbing his throat. "Sure are."

"Weren't you and your Nova Corps buddies just shooting at me? Didn't one of you just stab me in the leg?"

Dey shook his head. "No, they're not my buddies. And they're not Xandarian."

"Now I am super-confused," Vers said. "So if they're not Xandarians, why are they trying to kill me? And if you *are* a Xandarian, why are you trying to help me?"

"I should probably start at the beginning," Dey said.

"Probably." Vers felt a wave of nausea overcome her as her leg throbbed. Her foot was numb now—she tried to wiggle her toes but couldn't tell if they were moving or not. Probably not a great sign.

It didn't help that the comm-link had been dead now for almost a half hour. She hadn't heard anything from Starforce since the last interference-laden communication. The pain in her leg wouldn't stop, and Vers found herself replaying the last bit of chatter over in her head:

"*Leave her!*"

"*We're not leaving—*"

"*—not an option.*"

"*—compromised everything!*"

"*—don't trust . . .*"

Who were they talking about? Me? Do they think I'm some kind of traitor?

"You okay?"

Rhomann Dey's voice sliced right through Vers's thoughts. For a moment, she had forgotten where she was, or who she was with.

Not good.

"No, I'm not okay," Vers snapped. "I'm bleeding out. Start talking, before I decide to bleed all over you."

"That's really gross," Dey said, chuckling and then wincing at the pain the motion caused his still-raw throat. "Look, I know you won't believe me, but I really am here to help. I'm guessing you're here on a mission that your own government would disavow if you were to be captured?"

Vers said nothing, pinning Dey with a stony glare.

"I'll take your overwhelming response as a yes. I'm on the same kind of mission. Except you're here to steal something. And I'm here to make sure you steal it."

Now this is making absolutely no sense whatsoever.

"Say that again," Vers ordered.

"You're here to take the plans for the axiom cannon," Dey said. "You don't have to say anything, I know that's why you're here. And I know you already have the plans."

And he knows this how . . . ?

"There are elements in my government that believe we can force peace on the Kree through the use of this new weapon," Dey continued. "Those are the people who were shooting at you and stabbing you."

"And what part of the government do you

represent?" Vers questioned, rubbing her leg.

"I'm here on direct orders of Nova Prime," Dey said. "She believes that if both sides possess the same technology, then balance will be achieved, and we can have peace. She *wants* the Kree to have these plans."

"Then why not just give them to us?" Vers asked.

"She is not in the majority," Dey said. "But she's right. The axiom cannon is too powerful a weapon to be in the hands of any one entity. Its existence alone upsets the balance of power. And the temptation for one side to use it against another, knowing they could never retaliate, is too great."

Vers pondered Dey's words, silent. Then at last, she spoke. "So, you help me get out of here, which means fighting against your own side?"

Dey nodded.

"Wow. Your mission sucks more than mine."

CHAPTER 23

The ride through the upper atmosphere had been less than stellar. The Xandarian freighter had clearly seen better days—it was old, creaky, unreliable. Sun-Val sat at the controls, doing her best to bring the beater into line, and to deliver the ship and its crew through safely into the reaches of outer space.

"This is one heck of a ship you picked out," Sun-Val shouted over the roar of the engines. In order to increase the freighter's maximum flight speed, the vessel had been gutted. Anything that wasn't absolutely necessary to go from point A to point B while keeping anything inside alive was junked. That included all of the usual creature comforts like storage—save for a single weapons locker—padding, insulation, even seats. While it made the ship a good deal lighter, and therefore quicker, it also made traveling inside it an incredibly noisy and uncomfortable experience.

With the seats gone, the members of Starforce were strapped to the sides of the vessel. Every time the ship hit an air pocket on escape from the Kree home world's atmosphere, or experienced the flow of hot plasma bumping against its heat shield, the crew felt it.

Yon-Rogg turned his head to look toward the cockpit and at Sun-Val. "I didn't pick it out. That was all Korath," he yelled back.

In response, Korath snapped to attention. "It was all we could manage on such short notice," Korath shouted, his tone defensive. "It had the right markings, it had been registered properly—the Xandarians will never suspect. It's not my fault if it's not comfortable. Starforce isn't about comfort!"

Vers glanced over at Yon-Rogg and noticed

that her commander had what looked like the smallest beginnings of a grin on his face.

He's messing with Korath. Beautiful.

"You did well, Korath," Yon-Rogg said. "I was just . . . Vers, how would you say it?"

"He's busting your chops," Vers screamed. She never understood how she had gained all of these expressions that had somehow escaped her comrades. Maybe she just had one foot more in reality than they did.

Korath looked at her, cocking his head, right ear straining. "WHAT?!" he yelled, even louder.

Suddenly, the ship's engines cut out. As noisy as it had been just a fraction of a second before, it was now the exact opposite.

"I said, 'He's busting your chops,'" Vers repeated, her voice sounding at full decibel in the sudden quiet even though she was hardly speaking above a whisper now.

"Oh," Korath said, clearly not understanding the idiom.

"What did you think I said?" Vers asked.

Korath frowned. "It sounded like you said, 'He's lost in Skrull crops.'"

"What does *that* mean?" Bron-Char rumbled. "Why would she say something like that?"

Korath shrugged. "I don't know. That's why I didn't ask."

And they think I'm *unfocused.*

With the freighter at cruising speed, the various Starforce members unhooked their safety straps, freeing them from the walls of the ship's cargo hold. Now free to roam, they split up to oversee various tasks.

Att-Lass joined Minn-Erva, approaching the weapons locker to check on the various ordnance they would need on the mission to Sy'gyl. There were sniper rifles—Minn-Erva's specialty. There was an array of various pistols, the weapon favored by Att-Lass. Along with that were sundry edge weapons, like swords, knives, and Kree blades of all shapes and sizes.

Bron-Char wandered over to survey the

weapons, and gave a dry laugh. "Good luck with those," he thundered.

Minn-Erva shot Att-Lass a *Here we go again* look and rolled her eyes. He smiled.

"I'm just saying, they may be great for you, but these"—Bron-Char said, indicating his massive fists—"these are all I need."

"It's great to be you," Minn-Erva said drily.

Off to one side, Yon-Rogg conferred with Korath. Vers was about to approach them, when Sun-Val emerged from the ship's cockpit.

"It should be smooth sailing from here on out," Sun-Val announced, rubbing her hands together as if dusting them off. "Unless we run into the Nova Corps and they figure out we're not who we say we are."

"Power of positive thinking," Vers said.

"You're the new kid, right?" Sun-Val asked, turning to her with one eyebrow cocked.

Vers laughed. "How is it that it's the first time I'm meeting you, but *I'm* the new kid?" she asked, half-serious.

"Yon-Rogg told me about you," Sun-Val said. "Says you're pretty powerful."

"Yeah, well, let's hope so," Vers replied. "I guess we'll find out on this mission."

"It's a simple snatch and grab," Sun-Val said. "I've run plenty of these before. Don't worry about me, I'll be there for you and the crew when you're done. You just need to stay focused on the job."

Stay focused. Someone's been talking to Yon-Rogg.

"What's your story?" Vers asked as she checked on her uniform's comm-link.

"Not much to tell. Just your standard Kree pilot who will fly any mission . . . no questions asked," Sun-Val said, raising her eyebrows.

Point taken.

"Vers, come here," Yon-Rogg called from across the ship.

Vers felt a twinge of relief. The conversation with Sun-Val had taken a strange turn—Vers was getting a weird vibe off her, and it left her unsettled. "Well, great chatting," Vers said as she beat a hasty retreat. She felt Sun-Val's gaze on her back as she threaded her way toward her superiors, and had to stifle an involuntary shudder.

CHAPTER 24

"That's what I'm worried about. Those out-posts. There, and there," Yon-Rogg said, pointing at two separate areas on the holo-graphic map that hovered in the air before him.

"What are we looking at?" Vers asked, flick-ing a finger at the map.

"Sy'gyl," Korath said, dispassionately. "This is the compound we need to infiltrate. Specif-ically, *you* need to infiltrate."

As soon as the words left his lips, Yon-Rogg knew what was coming.

She'll pick up on it, he thought.

Vers looked at Korath, then at Yon-Rogg. "Me? But I thought—"

There we go.

"What did you think?" Korath interrupted, his tone suggesting annoyance.

"Well, I just thought that Att-Lass was our stealth expert," Vers continued. "If anyone has the skills necessary for infiltration, it's him. Wouldn't it make more sense to send him in? My abilities are a little . . . louder."

Korath exhaled deeply, as though Vers was an unruly child trying his patience, and glared at Yon-Rogg. The commander of Starforce turned to Vers, moving closer. "Then I suggest you practice being quiet," he said.

That decision sounded . . . final.

"I don't understand," Vers tried again. "That's all. I'll do my part, no questions asked, but—"

"Then why are you asking questions?" Korath asked.

"Well, you just asked a question," Vers retorted.

"I can ask all the questions I want, I'm second in command," Korath volleyed back.

There was a part of Yon-Rogg that actually took pleasure from the way Vers could needle Korath with just a few words. But as mission commander, he didn't have the luxury of showing it.

Yon-Rogg sighed. "Why don't you go back with the others and check on the weapons," he muttered to Korath. It wasn't a suggestion. Korath nodded sharply, gave Vers a prickly look, then headed to the weapons locker.

Now she's going to ask if she's in trouble.

"Am I in trouble?" Vers asked. "I feel like I'm in trouble."

"You have a lot to learn about following orders," Yon-Rogg said. "But no, you're not in trouble. I didn't want to say this in front of Korath, or the others, for that matter. But the decision to have you infiltrate the base on Sy'gyl comes from the highest level."

"Like, how high?" Vers inquired. "You mean, like . . . Supreme Intelligence high?"

The Supreme Intelligence was the ultimate leader of the Kree Empire. It combined

144

the vast knowledge of centuries' worth of the greatest Kree intellects. The ways of the Supreme Intelligence could be mysterious, but they weren't to be questioned. The Supreme Intelligence always acted in the best interests of the Kree Empire. Vers knew this. To suggest that it didn't know what it was doing was heresy of the highest order.

Yon-Rogg nailed her with a look. "The. Highest. Level."

"Understood," Vers said. Thoughts of her odd conversation with Sun-Val flew out of Vers's head as she considered the implications of what she was hearing. The Supreme Intelligence, demanding that Vers undertake a mission on her own?

"I wish you had more time to practice your . . . abilities," Yon-Rogg mused. "You're more powerful than you realize."

Vers smiled. "No, I realize just how powerful I am."

Yon-Rogg looked exasperated, but also as though he was trying to hold back a smile.

"You may just pull this off. Now pay close attention. . . ."

✦

"What were you and Yon-Rogg discussing up there?" Minn-Erva asked when Vers returned to the group.

Vers bent to inspect a sniper rifle. "Going over the lay of the land. He wants to talk with you next," Vers said. Though the woman's back was to her and her tone was casual, Minn-Erva could tell that she was hiding something.

Minn-Erva grabbed Vers's shoulder and wrenched her around. "It's not like him to go over the plan individually," she pushed. "We're a team. What one knows, we should all know."

"I'm sure he has his reasons for doing it this way," Bron-Char interjected, his deep, resonating voice bouncing off the walls of the cargo bay.

"Of course he does," Att-Lass added. "This is a real stealth mission. I'm sure he has separate objectives for each of us."

I don't like it. Vers is keeping something from us. "I'll be back," Minn-Erva said, ending the discussion. She placed the sniper rifle back into the weapons hold and locked it into place. "Anyone who touches that, dies." Then she stalked over to where Yon-Rogg was waiting.

"What's going on, Yon-Rogg?" she asked abruptly. *What did you tell Vers?*

Yon-Rogg met Minn-Erva's gaze, his face impassive. "When we disembark on Sy'gyl, we'll need you to cover the team. Everyone will fan out and take on their assigned tasks. You'll be in charge of keeping any potential hostiles off our backs."

Minn-Erva jerked her head, nodding sharply. "It's what I do," she said, her voice short. "What will Vers be doing?"

"While you watch our backs, and the rest of us clear a path, Vers will infiltrate the outpost, obtain the plans, and make it back to the freighter."

"Isn't that a job more suited to Att-Lass's talents?" Minn-Erva asked pointedly.

Yon-Rogg said nothing but gave a look at Minn-Erva that said, *Don't push me.*

Fine. I won't push. But I'll be watching Vers. Every step of the way.

CHAPTER 25

"Can you walk?" Dey asked Vers as they huddled on the surface of Sy'gyl.

"Of course I can walk," Vers said, her tone defensive as she rose to standing. But her body belied her intentions—the world suddenly went topsy-turvy, and Vers felt like her stomach was where her head should be, and vice versa. She staggered, braced herself against the stone wall, and held on. "Maybe not right this second."

"We're gonna have to move. The others will be here soon. And they're not gonna be nice like me," Dey said. He gestured to Vers, offering to give her some support so she could stand up.

She waved him off. Grimacing, she managed

to stand and keep upright this time. "I'm Kree," Vers said as she started to walk. "I don't need your help."

"Well, you kinda do, if you're gonna get out of here."

"Yeah, how's that?" Vers quipped.

"You're walking into a minefield, for one thing."

Vers stopped in her tracks and turned to look at Dey. She had only gone a few steps into the field littered with debris. But still.

"You could have said something before I started walking," Vers chided.

"Not like you gave me any warning," Dey said. "Just walk backward, retracing your steps. I mean, step where you stepped—"

"Thanks, I think I got it," Vers said, annoyed. She took one step at a time, trying her best to match the footprints she had just left in the dirt. Several seconds and one deep breath later, Vers was back to where she had started. "How did you know this area was mined?"

"I mined it," Dey said, pointing in the opposite direction. "Let's go this way."

<hr />

"The comm-link is dead. I can't get anything on it," Minn-Erva said, chucking it to the ground in frustration. She, Att-Lass, and Korath had made it back to the freighter without incident. They were just missing Yon-Rogg, Bron-Char, and Vers.

Vers. What the hell is she up to?

It had been an hour, maybe a little less, since she had lost contact with Vers. It was supposed to be simple. Easy. Snatch and grab. It had turned out to be anything but.

"I'm telling you, the mission has been compromised," Minn-Erva insisted. "She should have been here by now, with the plans. Either they got her, or she's one of them."

"Are you trying to tell me that Vers is working for Xandar now?" Att-Lass said in disbelief. "Do you honestly think that?"

"After everything that's happened, I don't know what to think," Minn-Erva replied.

"One of you better get in there and prep the ship," Korath said, his voice flat.

"What about Yon-Rogg and Bron-Char?" Att-Lass asked.

"The last communication they got off said they'd be meeting us at fourteen hundred hours. That's coming up," Korath said. "Either they'll be here, or they won't."

"Are you saying we should leave without them? Without Vers?" Att-Lass protested.

"Vers, who knows? Yon-Rogg and Bron-Char will be here. And I am saying that we are Starforce and we will follow our orders. To. The. Letter," Korath said, laying down the law.

"I'll go inside and get the ship ready," Minn-Erva said. "Something tells me we're going to need to bug out of here in a hurry."

The leg was bothering her more than it had before. Vers bit the inside of her cheek so hard, she tasted copper. Blood.

Wonder how much blood I'm losing.

"Where's your extraction point?" Dey asked. They had made their way out of the bombed-out foundation and into a nearby copse of trees.

Vers stopped walking for a moment, bent over, and placed her hands on her knees. She took a deep breath, then looked around. "About three clicks in that direction," she said, pointing northeast. "Give or take."

"I think we're gonna have to take care of that leg before we go any farther, or you're not gonna make it," Dey observed.

"You a doctor?"

"No," Dey said.

"Then you're not getting anywhere near this leg."

"I *am* trained in combat medicine," Dey said. "If you let me look at it, I can probably at least stop the bleeding. Y'know, so you don't pass out. Or die."

Pass out or die. Bad and worse. These options stink.

Despite her better instincts, Vers sat down on the sparse grass. It felt good to take weight off the injured leg. She leaned her back against a tree and exhaled in relief, feeling more grounded with the firm support backing her. "I suppose if you were going to kill me, you would have done it by now."

"I'm going to take that as a 'Yes, Rhomann Dey, please look at my leg and see if there's anything you can do.'"

"Yeah, sure, whatever," Vers murmured, her eyes beginning to close. "Yes, Rhomann Dey, please—"

But before she could finish repeating the sentence, everything went black, taking Vers back to the journey that had brought Starforce to Sy'gyl in the first place.

CHAPTER 26

"Buckle up! It's gonna be a bumpy ride," Vers shouted. Korath just looked at her.

"Of course it's going to be bumpy," he said, as if he couldn't believe she had stated the obvious. "We're under attack!"

Just seconds before, the freighter had been making its way to the edge of Xandarian space. So far, so good. There had been no incidents. Casual contact had been made with at least one Nova vessel. IDs had been exchanged, registration numbers run.

No problems.

Until now, when they were being fired upon by a hostile force.

Minn-Erva turned her head to look toward

the cockpit. "I hope she's as good a pilot as Yon-Rogg says she is," Minn-Erva muttered, loud enough that Yon-Rogg could hear. The leader of Starforce shot her a look.

Good. You were supposed to hear that.

Sun-Val was at the controls, and even in the cargo hold, over the din of the engines whining and straining, Minn-Erva could hear her shouting and cursing in her struggle to outmaneuver the threat. The freighter wasn't a sleek warship. It wasn't designed for dogfights, for taking a beating or delivering one.

"Hey! They're our guys!"

"What's that?" Yon-Rogg shouted, trying to be heard above the omnipresent noise.

Sun-Val craned her head back, mouth turned toward the cargo bay, eyes still looking ahead. "They're ours! Kree fighters! They're identifying us as Xandarian!"

Minn-Erva scoffed. "Of course they are. We're in a Xandarian ship. And we can't tell them who we are, or the Xandarians will pick up the chatter, and the mission will be over before it begins."

"What do we do?" Att-Lass asked.

"I say we fire back," Vers said. All eyes turned toward her.

"Do what, now?" Minn-Erva barked.

"She's right," Yon-Rogg seconded, surprising everyone. "If we don't fire back, we raise suspicion on both sides. That's the only way to get through this in one piece. Sun-Val!"

"I hear ya, boss! What do you want me to do?" the pilot shouted.

"Fire! All weapons!" Yon-Rogg ordered.

There was a slight pause, then everyone in the cargo bay heard Sun-Val say, "Well, we only have the one on this heap, but I'll go ahead and fire it anyway."

The freighter lurched slightly as Sun-Val activated the freighter's lone cannon. The blast nearly tore the small ship apart as sparks rained down from the cables that crisscrossed the ceiling. A panel next to Bron-Char's head exploded, the metal plate narrowly missing the warrior's massive head.

"Did we fire, or did we get hit?" Vers asked.

"That is a good question," Minn-Erva acknowledged grudgingly.

I can't believe the two of us actually agree on something.

"I want to say that was us firing," Att-Lass said.

"I think that was us firing, too," Bron-Char added.

"What was that?" Yon-Rogg bellowed at the cockpit.

Sun-Val yanked on the controls, pulling the freighter hard to the left. The entire ship wobbled ominously as another metal panel popped off the wall near Att-Lass and fire broke out from behind. "That," shouted Sun-Val, "was us getting hit. That thing before? That was us firing."

"How long until we enter Xandarian-occupied space?" Korath asked, his voice taut.

"Not too long now," Sun-Val said. "About a minute!"

We may not be alive in one minute.

Minn-Erva felt the ship jerk, this time to the right. Her body was thrown against the straps, which dug into her shoulders and chest.

"Almost there!" Sun-Val yelled from the cockpit. "Incoming!"

The next blast ripped into the freighter, taking a small chunk of the hull with it. A hole had opened, exposing the cargo bay to the cold void of space beyond. Immediately, the effects of decompression could be felt as the atmosphere within the ship was sucked out to fill the near vacuum outside.

"I'm on it!" Someone would have to reach the shield to seal off the breach before the team either asphyxiated or got sucked out into space. Minn-Erva struggled with her harness. The freighter was bucking back and forth, and started to roll, making it almost impossible to disengage the safety catch.

Whipping her head down, Minn-Erva saw Vers drop from her harness, slamming against the ceiling—which, the way the ship was rolling, was now the floor. Pulling herself along the sparking electrical cables that crossed the ceiling, Vers made her way to the breach and slammed her hand on the shield's button.

At once, a luster of shimmering green-hued energy appeared, covering the tear in the freighter's hull. Space was still visible beyond, but the shield would prevent more of the ship's atmosphere from leaking into the void.

Minn-Erva dropped back against the wall, no longer fighting her harness. There was no need.

She did it.

"And we're clear!" Sun-Val shouted. At last, the pilot brought the freighter under control. No longer being shot at by the Kree ships, Sun-Val slowed the ship's roll, righting the vessel.

"We're in Xandarian space?" Bron-Char queried.

"That's affirmative," Sun-Val responded.

"Then we're on our way," Yon-Rogg said.

"Nice work, Vers," he called across the bay. Vers just shrugged.

Minn-Erva observed the exchange, torn between jealousy, relief, and admiration. Was it possible she had misjudged Vers after all?

CHAPTER 27

"Orbit achieved."

Vers looked out of the cockpit at the planet Sy'gyl below. It was a cold-looking world, not at all like the Kree home world. Or like the planet Xandar, for that matter.

"Welcome to Sy'gyl," Sun-Val said, as if she were some kind of interstellar tour guide, and not the pilot of what was essentially a top secret suicide mission. "Temperatures on the surface range from ninety to one hundred twenty degrees. Nice and hot, for those who like that sort of thing. Internal core is unstable, resulting in occasional earthquakes, volcanic eruptions, and so on."

"Sounds like a great place to take a vacation," Vers muttered.

"What's a vacation?" Korath asked.

"Exactly," Vers quipped. Korath sent her a mystified look, as usual.

"Okay. Two minutes until we break orbit and enter Sy'gyl's atmosphere," Yon-Rogg said, prepping his team. "When we land, we hit the ground running. There won't be much time. Everyone knows their part. Play it."

"What do we do if we encounter any Xandarian resistance?" Vers asked.

"Don't encounter any," Yon-Rogg replied.

"What do you mean, 'don't encounter any'?" Minn-Erva said. "Of course there's going to be resistance! Do you mean don't take a shot? Don't defend ourselves?"

"She does make a good point," Att-Lass said.

"Damn right I do," Minn-Erva spat.

Vers nodded in agreement. "Yon-Rogg, I understand the nature of the mission, but—"

"As far as the Kree Empire is concerned, we are not here. And as far as the Xandarian government knows, we are not here. We are not here," Yon-Rogg elucidated. "That means we are to be invisible. Leave no trace. No clues. No indication that Starforce ever set foot on Sy'gyl."

Maybe telling us earlier would have been a good idea.

"Is that understood?" Yon-Rogg asked, but it was clear that he wasn't really asking. He was telling.

As always, Starforce replied, "Yes, sir," nearly in unison.

The brief trip from the orbit around Sy'gyl to its surface was just how Yon-Rogg liked it—dull and uneventful. The freighter landed at the predetermined point, just on the outskirts of a mountainous region that was, for all intents and purposes, unpopulated.

Save for a fortresslike structure located in a

crater in the middle of the mountain range of Nar'dath.

That's where we're going. Where she's going, Yon-Rogg thought. *I don't know what the Supreme Intelligence's point is in having the most powerful member of Starforce break and enter like a thief, but I'm not going to question it.*

When the freighter touched down, Yon-Rogg unbuckled and moved over to the ship's hatch. Turning, he looked at the members of Starforce, who had all disengaged their harnesses and were now looking to their leader.

"Only Minn-Erva takes a weapon," Yon-Rogg said. "She's covering everyone. All others, leave your weapons here."

Minn-Erva stood near the weapons locker and removed the sniper rifle. She checked its chamber to make sure it was loaded. Then she removed a bandolier full of rounds and slung it across her left shoulder.

"Minn-Erva," Yon-Rogg said, looking at his best sniper. "You'll cover our approach

to the facility. Fire only if necessary. Everyone else, it's your job to make sure it won't be
necessary."

"What's my job, boss?" Sun-Val asked,
peering into the cargo hold from the cockpit.

"You stay here with the ship," Yon-Rogg
said. "Any sign of trouble, you take off."

"What about you guys?"

"We'll manage," Vers said, almost reading
Yon-Rogg's mind. Yon-Rogg gave a grunt of
approval and turned to lead the team from the
ship.

We'll manage. It's what we do.

"This place is hot. Capital *H*, capital *O*, capital
T, hot," Att-Lass said, trudging along the stony
Sy'gyllian ground. Fissures in the planet's surface vented hot gas from time to time, filling
everyone's noses with the smell of methane
and sulfur and who knows what else. Flames
flicked upward from behind a rocky ridge just
beyond where they stood.

The sky was very nearly red.

"Join Starforce, see the world," Vers said, laughing to herself.

"Something funny?" Minn-Erva asked sharply.

"No, not really," Vers replied. "Just trying to make light of a very dark situation."

"Cut the chatter," Yon-Rogg said from behind. "Until we establish the location of the enemy, use hand signals."

Bron-Char nodded and swiveled his head around, looking at the fiery surroundings. Something appeared to catch his eye, and he motioned for everyone to stop.

The members of Starforce froze in their tracks, all eyes on Bron-Char. He raised his hand, indicating something was just ahead.

Yon-Rogg's eyes sought out Att-Lass, who met his leader's gaze. With a jerk of his head, Yon-Rogg ordered Att-Lass to investigate. Quietly, the stealthy warrior ran forward, relying on the boulders that dotted the surface for cover. Att-Lass soon disappeared from sight.

No one said a word or moved so much as a muscle. They stood their ground, waiting. The sound of hot gasses escaping from cracks in the ground could be heard, as well as the crackle of fire in the background.

Where is he . . . ? What's going on?

Yon-Rogg looked over his shoulder, back toward the freighter. There was no going back. He wasn't going to leave Sy'gyl without the plans. He would not fail. Not today.

Not ever.

The sound of rapid footsteps brought Yon-Rogg back, as he saw Att-Lass running toward them. Att-Lass moved his right hand, flashing the *okay* sign.

"What was it?" Yon-Rogg asked in a hushed voice.

"Ship."

"Xandarian?"

Att-Lass nodded. "Nova."

We're in deep now.

CHAPTER 28

Vers gasped awake, jolting out of her unconscious reverie, and almost immediately wished she hadn't. *My head hurts.*

My leg hurts.

No, scratch that. EVERYTHING hurts.

Vers blinked, her eyes opening slowly, letting in the light. She found it hard to focus, no matter how much she tried.

What's wrong? Why can't I focus, why—?

"You're awake. Good."

Vers blinked again, trying to get her eyes to register her surroundings. But she recognized the voice immediately.

Rhomann Dey.

"Do I still have a leg?" Vers asked, only half joking.

"Sure do," the Xandarian replied. "In fact, you have two of 'em. One's in better shape than the other."

"I bet," Vers said. The shadowy image before her slowly started to coalesce until it became decidedly more personlike.

"How long was I out?" Vers asked, tentatively reaching down to feel her leg. She saw that the tourniquet was gone, and in its place, a proper bandage. The leg still hurt like mad. But the throbbing was nearly gone, meaning that Dey must have found a way to stem the bleeding.

"I don't know, fifteen minutes, maybe," Dey said, checking on Vers's leg. "I did what I could. You're gonna need to have that taken care of when you get back to your ship. Assuming you have a medic with you."

Yeah, I'm not telling you anything about who—or what—I have with me.

"I know, I know, you can't tell me anything,"

Dey added as though reading her mind, holding up his hands in mock surrender.

"Not like there's anything you don't know already," Vers shot back.

Dey didn't respond, just gave her a long look. Then he smiled. "I gave you something for the pain," Dey said. "You should be able to get back on your feet."

Still slumped against the tree, Vers grabbed on to the trunk and pulled herself up. To her surprise, she was able to put some weight on the injured leg.

"You did good," she said, looking at Dey.

"I do what I can."

"You smell something?" Vers asked.

Dey sniffed the air around them, then his eyes went wide. "I think we have a problem," he said, pointing behind Vers.

Whipping her head around, Vers saw exactly what Dey meant. A blaze had broken out in the distance—no doubt a fissure had opened, spewing volcanic gas and lava, setting fire to the trees that grew in the area. The fire was now spreading from tree to tree, flames leaping, jumping.

"It was nice while it lasted," Vers said.

⚜

They moved through the forest as fast as Vers's injured leg would let them, staying ahead of the rapidly spreading flames as Dey navigated them through the winding foliage.

A Xandarian helping a Kree. Now I've seen everything.

"Where do we go from here?" Vers asked.

Dey looked down at his wrist, swiping a finger, obviously looking at a small screen. "If we can make it to the edge of this forest, it says there's a clearing, all rocks," Dey observed. "Flames shouldn't be able to follow. Then we get a breather, and get you back to your ship."

"Why are you helping me?" Vers asked as they ducked under a tree limb.

"I told you why," Dey said. "Orders."

"I don't mean your orders," Vers said. "I mean, you're a Nova. I'm a Kree warrior.

Shouldn't we be, like, killing each other or something?"

Dey looked at Vers as they continued to move along. "I don't really believe in killing someone if I don't have to."

"You've never killed anyone before, have you?" Vers asked.

"I guess I don't really believe in killing, period," Dey said. "Was it that obvious?"

"Yeah," Vers said. "That's not a bad thing."

"What? Not bad that it's obvious, or not bad that I don't believe in killing?"

"Both."

The two were nearing the edge of the forest, the rocky clearing now visible just beyond. They had come to a large tree stump that had to be at least the size of a small building. It was enormous. But where was the rest of it?

Vers looked over her shoulder as she saw the flames continue to grow, consuming tree after tree. They were almost in the clear. The thought that they might have been caught in the blaze if she had been unconscious even just a few minutes longer sent a slight chill down the base of her neck.

"Down!"

Before Vers had a chance to look, she felt Rhomann Dey's hand slam into the small of her back, shoving her to the mossy ground below. He landed right next to her as a blast of energy flashed in front of them. The blast razed the ground about an inch in front of where Vers's left hand had come to rest.

Looking up, she saw it. At the top of a stump, a gleam of silver against the bloodred sky. A weapon. And holding the weapon, a Xandarian warrior.

"He's not Nova," Dey said.

"How can you tell?"

"A Nova doesn't shoot first before asking questions," he replied shortly.

"How about second? Do they shoot second?" Vers asked, as they both hugged the ground for cover.

CHAPTER 29

The approach to the Nar'dath pass had been as though traversing through a literal hell. Flames erupted on either side of Starforce as they climbed over boulders, the smell of sulfur threatening to overwhelm them. Att-Lass had continued to take point on recon, and was scampering up to the top of a peak. Below him, Yon-Rogg, Korath, Bron-Char, and Vers waited.

Looking out from his vantage point, Att-Lass cast his eyes downward, back to Yon-Rogg, then flashed a hand, signaling all-clear.

Yon-Rogg motioned for the others to follow after Att-Lass. One by one, they scrambled up the rock wall, grabbing on to handholds and deftly swinging their feet to join Att-Lass at the top. As quietly as he could, Yon-Rogg spoke into his comm-link: "You getting all this?"

There was a brief hiss of static, and then a voice responded, "Got it. You're covered all the way to the approach."

Minn-Erva. Yon-Rogg looked around and didn't see her anywhere, but he knew that his prized sniper was perched somewhere nearby, taking everything into view. At the slightest hint of trouble, she could drop an enemy and give Starforce the chance they needed to pull off their mission.

But we're not going to let it come to that.

The team assembled at the peak, their bodies flattened out among the rocks. Yon-Rogg swiped at his wrist, and a holographic diagram appeared. Vers looked at the image, and then down the peak into the crater below—an exact match. It was a concrete bunker, with no characteristic markings. There were no windows and only two doors, on opposite sides of the bunker. What's more, there didn't appear to be anyone outside the facility.

"There's no way it's this easy," Vers whispered.

"Sometimes it is," Att-Lass said, softly.

"Let's assume this will be difficult," Yon-Rogg interjected.

"Makes sense," Vers replied. "That way everyone's happy."

Korath glared at Vers. "Are you going to take this seriously or not?"

"She knows how serious it is," Yon-Rogg said, cutting off Korath. Then he looked at Vers as if to say, *You DO know how serious this is, yes?*

Vers gave one short nod and remained quiet.

"Okay, then. Vers. Make your way down. Enter the compound. The plans are on Level Three," Yon-Rogg instructed.

"How will I know where to look, exactly?" Vers asked.

Fingers dancing on his wrist, Yon-Rogg

produced another holographic image of a bespectacled woman with no hair. "Peer Kaal, scientist. It's her project. Find her, get the plans, get out."

Vers's eyes widened as she took in the image of Peer Kaal, committing it to memory. Without saying a word, she took a series of short, shallow breaths and started to move down from the peak, toward the compound in the crater below.

The comm-link crackled to life. "Don't screw this up," Minn-Erva said.

"Thanks for the vote of confidence," Vers retorted, and turned to leave.

Yon-Rogg watched as Vers advanced closer and closer to the compound beneath the team. *She can do this. I know she can do this.*

❋

SKKKRRAAAAAK. "Still all clear, no sign of the enemy," Minn-Erva said over the comm-link.

Vers was nearly at the rim of the crater. So far, there had been no sign of any enemy activity whatsoever. No outposts; not so much as a sensor that registered on any of Starforce's scanning equipment. Whatever the Xandarians were making here, they were doing so in utmost secrecy, hoping that the place they chose was so remote, and so inhospitable, that no one would ever think to look there.

It was too bad they'd underestimated their Kree enemies.

"At the edge," Vers replied. "I'm about fifty meters from the entrance to the compound. I don't see anyone."

KKRRSSSAAAAK. "All clear, you're good to go," Minn-Erva said.

You trust her, right, Vers? Like, she's not going to lead you into the middle of a firefight just because she has some weird grudge against you, right?

Vers tried to get that thought out of her mind.

Stay focused.

But her mind was in overdrive, thoughts of her team intercutting with her lingering misgivings about Sun-Val and the strange feeling their conversation had given her. She hardly knew the pilot. Yon-Rogg trusted her, and that should have been good enough. But it wasn't.

She could hear Yon-Rogg's voice echoing around her head. Vers didn't know why, but sometimes it was difficult for her to center herself in the present. It was like there was some thought that she couldn't quite grab, but was somehow drawing her attention anyway. She was unable to put her finger on it, wasn't even sure if there WAS an "it."

And now's not the time to be thinking about this.

Vers rose from her position behind a large, fire-scorched rock. Pumping her legs, she sprinted, covering the distance between the rock and the entrance to the compound in mere seconds. Slamming her back against the concrete bunker, she spoke quietly and calmly into the comm-link, "I'm goin' in."

ZZZAAAAAKKKK. "Good luck."

Did Minn-Erva just wish me good luck? This day just gets weirder and weirder.

From her perch nestled between two boulders, Minn-Erva watched through her scope as Vers entered the concrete bunker below. The bunker had no doors to speak of, just the two openings on opposite sides.

She wasn't sure if she trusted Vers entirely. Vers had always been different from the others, and the way she had caught Yon-Rogg's immediate attention had admittedly never sat well with Minn-Erva. But that didn't really matter now. Everyone had their role, and Minn-Erva's was to safeguard the members of her team. Vers's was to snatch and grab a set of plans that would change the balance of power between the Kree and the Xandarians.

SKRRAAAKKK. "Any word from Vers?" came the voice over the comm-link.

Yon-Rogg.

Minn-Erva activated the comm-link on her end and said, "She's going in. Haven't heard anything else."

ZZSSSSKKK—"may not be able to get a"—*ZZAKKKK*—"signal inside that bunker," Yon-Rogg offered.

Minn-Erva didn't respond. She stayed focused, eye on the scope and on the bunker, looking for any sign of activity. The lives of five people were depending on it.

Then, she saw it.

Or rather, them.

"Five o'clock," Minn-Erva said over the comm-link, indicating the position of the bogey. "Three subjects, all wearing Nova gear."

ZAARRKKKK. "See them," Yon-Rogg replied. "Bron-Char, you're with me. We'll keep an eye on them. Korath, Att-Lass, you stay here in case anyone else decides to show up."

Minn-Erva adjusted her scope and repositioned. *And now things get interesting. . . .*

CHAPTER 30

SKKKRAAAAKKK. "You stay here in case anyone else decides to show up."

The voice crackled loud over the freighter's communications system, as Sun-Val focused on trying to repair the breach in the hull from the misguided Kree attack. At first glance, she had hoped that the damage looked worse than it actually was. But as she got closer and actually started to do the work, she saw just how bad things were. And how bad they could get.

"This whole thing is shot," Sun-Val muttered to herself. She removed an interior panel next to the breach to get a better look at the shield circuitry that had provided the temporary patch during the earlier Kree attack.

It was fried. Sun-Val shook her head in disbelief. It was a minor miracle that the shield had worked at all. If the ship had sustained any more damage in that area, the shields wouldn't have come to life when Vers slammed the button.

And it would have been bye-bye, Starforce.

Sun-Val stood up and walked to the back of the cargo hold. Though the freighter had been stripped down to the bare essentials, there were still a few things left on board in case of emergency. Two extra hull plates, for example. Sun-Val examined them. They weren't made of the same heavy-duty materials as the originals, but they would make do. At least, it would enable them to make it back to the Kree home world.

Providing no one decides to shoot at us again.

She took one of the panels by either side and hefted it upward. Then she walked over to the hull breach and nestled it into place. It wasn't a perfect fit, but with some hammering, some welding, and a lot of cursing, Sun-Val figured she could get everything in working order by the time Starforce completed their mission.

"Let's get it on," Sun-Val said to no one in particular, and fired up the welding gun from her toolbox.

Her eyes were focused on the light blue flame coming from the tip of the welding gun, as Sun-Val ran it along the top edge of the metal plate. It was a slow process; she had to make sure that every inch had been welded tight. When she was done, she'd have to go over everything at a microscopic level, to ensure that the patch would hold.

Once again, the comm-link came to life. *SKKAARRRK.* "Att-Lass, Korath—I don't have Yon-Rogg or Bron-Char in sight. Anything on your end?"

Sun-Val listened as she did her work. Her job was to pilot the ship, nothing else. So this was more like listening to some kind of audio-only drama program play out than like something that was actually happening. At least, that's how she thought of it.

ZZZRRAAKKKK. "Negative, nothing on this end. Korath out."

Almost done with this edge . . .

A half hour later, Sun-Val had finished the patch. It wasn't her best work, she decided, but it also wasn't her worst.

She wiped the line of sweat that had developed on her brow, and walked out of the freighter's hatch to survey her work outside. The patch looked good from this angle; it would hold.

It'd better hold, or we're in trouble. I'm in trouble.

SNAP!

Suddenly a sharp noise broke the silence that surrounded the freighter. It sounded like something breaking—like a tree branch, or a stick. Sun-Val looked at the stand of trees that stood to one side of the freighter. On the other side, there were only rocks and the flames erupting from the fissures between the cracks.

With all that fire, how is it that this planet even HAS trees? And why are you thinking about that right now?

Sun-Val scanned the tree line but couldn't see anything. Just as she turned her attention back to the patch, she heard the same loud *SNAP* again.

Reaching down to a pouch on her belt, Sun-Val withdrew a small pistol. She knew that Yon-Rogg had told Starforce "no weapons," but she decided that since she technically wasn't a member of Starforce, that rule must not apply to her. Approaching the woods, Sun-Val held the pistol in her right hand, using her left to steady her aim. She took cautious steps, one foot in front of the other, eyes darting back and forth, looking for any sign of movement.

Yon-Rogg had specifically requested for Sun-Val to pilot the mission from the Kree's range of expert pilots, and not just because of her incredible flying skills. Sun-Val was also a skilled marksman and an expert on rough-terrain combat. Most pilots weren't. Yon-Rogg had made it clear in her briefing that, while her core role in this operation was to pilot the freighter, she might be called upon in dire need to provide backup to the Starforce team.

To Sun-Val, suspicious sounds coming from an indeterminate location qualified as dire.

She knew that Yon-Rogg trusted her implicitly, as did Korath. The others? She wasn't so sure. The way Vers kept looking at her. Why did the warrior seem so suspicious of her?

Sun-Val rolled up her left sleeve, revealing a wrist control unit. With a few swipes of her fingers, she activated the freighter's hatch, sealing it shut.

Don't want any unwelcome guests waiting for me when I get back.

Taking aim once more, Sun-Val walked into the forest.

CHAPTER 31

"We're in trouble," Dey said, looking up at their assailant. "He's got the high g—"

"Do not complete that thought," Vers interrupted. "I get it."

A series of blasts from the weapon above seared the ground between Dey and Vers.

"Whoever this is, I think he's playing with us," Dey said with a grimace.

Don't do it. Yon-Rogg said not to do it; you know better than this. Try using your brains, instead of letting your emotions get the better of you.

"Then let's play back," Vers said, a smile on her face as she ignored the little voice that was screaming inside her head. *Sorry, Yon-Rogg. You know I can't resist a chance to emote.*

"Not sure I follow," Dey replied, keeping his head down.

"I recommend you don't" was Vers's reply. Without warning, she stood up straight, her body an inviting target for the sniper perched atop the enormous stump above. She saw the glint of light bounce off the barrel of the enemy's weapon, saw that it was now pointing directly at her. Vers raised her hands, making fists, until both arms were outstretched fully. As if aiming, she pointed her fists at what she thought was the right angle.

"What are you d—?" Dey began.

And then Vers let loose. Her body glowed, power gathering from all through her and centering itself in her fists. A microsecond later, photon energy erupted from her hands, following a straight line, until the blast reached the top of the stump. There was an explosion, then a scream. Fire erupted where the photon blast had struck.

The assailant fell from the top of the stump, landing on the ground below with a dull thud.

The body wasn't moving, but Vers could see that whoever it was, he was still breathing.

Then Vers turned to look at Dey, and smiled.

"Problem solved," Vers said simply.

"How did you do that?" Dey said, standing up, pointing at Vers's hands. "With the hands, the thing . . ."

Vers glanced downward at her hands. His was a question she often asked herself more than she liked to let on. "I'm not sure. I mean, I don't remember how. . . . It's just something I can do."

Dey scratched his head. "It's pretty good."

Vers nodded. "Comes in handy. But it also draws a crowd. If anyone was with this guy, I'm sure we've alerted them to our presence."

"I think they already knew we were here," Dey said. "Someone must have tipped them off."

"How?" Vers asked. "We landed well out of scanning range. Total stealth approach."

"Not important now. I'll tell you later," Dey said.

Unfortunately for Dey, that wasn't how Vers worked. "How about you tell me now, or I fry you?" Vers said, wiggling the fingers on her right hand.

"Fine," Dey said as he walked toward the stump, and the body that lay at its base. "Take a look at this guy."

Vers followed next to Dey. Her assessment from afar had been accurate—he was still breathing, but unconscious from the fall, his body charred somewhat from her blast. The man was wearing Xandarian garb, but there was something strange about his features. They seemed malleable somehow, almost like his face was . . . melting.

Did I do that to him?

"You didn't do that to him," Dey said, as if reading her mind. "Just watch."

Vers kept looking, and a second later, the unconscious man's features began to morph once more, until the skin took on a green-ish hue. The ears became pointy, and below the bottom lip little vertical ridges began to develop, like small creases.

"A Skrull!" Vers said, surprised at the sound of shock in her own voice.

"A Skrull," Dey echoed. "Right now, you're probably saying to yourself, 'Hey, what's really going on here?'"

Darn right I am.

"Something like that," Vers said.

"They arrived shortly before you did," Dey said. "I tracked them as they came in. I'm assuming they're here for the same reason that you are, to steal the plans for the axiom cannon."

"And because he tried to just kill us outright, you knew it was a Skrull?" Vers asked.

"I had a pretty good idea," Dey replied.

"How many more of them are there?"

"One more," Dey said. "I saw two leave their ship. They were flying under Xandarian colors."

Glad to see we weren't the only ones with the same brilliant plan. I'll have to tell Yon-Rogg. . . .

"We have to get back to the freighter," Vers said. For the first time in a while, she felt the return of the dull throbbing sensation in her injured leg. Whatever Dey had given her was starting to wear off. Vers gritted her teeth. If only she had listened to her instincts and turned around right when she'd entered the bunker. Willing a distraction from the ever-growing pain, Vers thought back to those first steps.

This is by far the creepiest mission I've ever been on.

CHAPTER 32

As Vers entered the concrete bunker, she was surprised to find it was almost completely empty. It was also dark, filled with smoke and gas that was making her eyes tear. She raised her right hand to cover her mouth and nose, and blinked her eyes several times to clear them.

Neither worked very well.

It was difficult to see inside with all the smoke, but Vers was sure that she had caught a glimpse of a small rock located by a far wall near the corner. That was the only discerning feature of the bunker, as far as she could tell. It could mean nothing. Or it could be the only way into whatever was going on here.

If anyone's watching, I doubt they can see a thing through this smoke. So here goes . . .

She crept over toward the small rock that she had seen, moving along the wall, trying to keep as low a profile as possible, the rush of the mission making her feel bold and strong, like always.

Reaching for the small rock, Vers tried to pick it up. It wouldn't budge. But as far as she could tell, it wasn't attached to the floor. It just seemed to be sitting there. So why couldn't she lift it?

Kneeling down, Vers examined the rock more closely. She noticed a small circular groove that surrounded the rock, like the floor around it had been worn away by something being turned repeatedly.

Something being turned . . .

Placing her hand on the rock, Vers tried to turn the rock clockwise. It wouldn't budge. Then she tried to turn it counterclockwise.

The rock practically spun in answer.

A few seconds later, the rock stopped turning, and Vers saw a small circular section of the floor sink into the ground.

One hidden entrance, coming up.

Without pausing, Vers jumped into the hole in the ground.

Vers landed hard on the surface below. She saw that she was inside a tunnel. The floor was lined with tile, as were the walls. There were dim yellow lights embedded in the ceiling, every five meters or so. The hallway seemed to stretch on into the distance forever. There were doors along either side of the hallway, all unmarked.

"I'm in," Vers said, whispering over her comm-link.

All she could hear in response was static.

Can't get any reception underground. Great, again . . .

Slowly, carefully, Vers walked down the hall, sticking to the right side, pressing her back against the wall as she moved along. She looked down every few seconds to make sure she wasn't stepping on anything, activating any hidden alarms.

She came to the first door on her right. There was no window. The only way to find out what lay beyond was to open it and go inside. She pressed her hand on the door and was surprised as it automatically whooshed downward, into the floor.

Vers set one foot inside the room, and an automatic overhead light activated. She could see a desk, an old cot, and a cabinet with a sink. There was a shelf lined with books on one wall. The space looked like someone's living quarters. All that was missing was the dismal little room's inhabitant.

Stepping back into the hallway, Vers watched as right away the door zoomed upward upon her exit. She looked down the hallway, noting two doors on the left-hand side, another door on the right, and a door at the end.

Which door are you hiding behind, Peer Kaal?

Vers had made it to the end of the hallway. She'd opened three more doors—the two on the left, and one on the right. She found one room filled with equipment, another that resembled a computer lab, and a small proving ground seemingly used for experiments of some kind.

That left the door at the very end. And either Peer Kaal was there, or she wasn't. And if she wasn't there, the mission would be a wash.

She made it to the last door, and Vers placed her hand in the middle. It slid downward.

"I knew you would come," said a voice.

Vers looked in and saw a bald-headed woman seated behind a pile of machinery, glasses resting on her forehead.

"Peer Kaal?" Vers asked.

"Peer Kaal," the scientist answered as she quickly rose from behind her work and practically ran over to Vers. She grabbed Vers by her shoulders and shook her vigorously. "I'm glad you are here. Perhaps now we can end this madness."

Vers took Kaal's hands, removing them from her shoulders. "That's what I'm here for. Do you have the plans?"

Kaal looked at Vers. "I *am* the plans."

CHAPTER 33

"Att-Lass, Korath—do you copy? Come in, do you copy?"

Static was her only answer.

Minn-Erva squatted in her perch, shifting her weight from left leg to right and back again in an effort to stave off the pins-and-needles feeling that had crept in after the first hour. But she had little choice. With Yon-Rogg and Bron-Char keeping tabs on the three Nova officers, it was up to Minn-Erva to keep the compound secure and stay on top of Att-Lass and Korath, who were still down there somewhere.

Even if the comm-links appeared to become

essentially worthless once Starforce descended from the mountaintop.

Peering into the scope, Minn-Erva checked out the two openings to the concrete bunker. No sign of movement. Beyond the crater, on the other side, she could just make out the tops of trees. Aside from the sound of gas erupting from fissures, it was relatively quiet.

I hate it when it gets quiet.

As it turned out, Minn-Erva didn't have to suffer the silence for very long. A high-pitched sound suddenly assaulted her ears, causing an intense ringing and an immediate headache. She fought off the impulse to press her fingertips to her temples, keeping her hands on her weapon and her eye on the scope.

Minn-Erva swiveled her head back and forth, moving the scope along with her, to see if she could pinpoint the source of the unpleasant noise. She didn't see anyone, and there appeared to be no movement on the ground below.

Then she glanced upward.

Hovering in the sky just above was what almost looked like a bird. It was small, with two wings. But Minn-Erva knew that it wasn't a bird.

It was a stealth bomb. But stealth bombs weren't in the Xandarians' arsenal—they were the tools of mercenaries and some of the more warlike planetary governments throughout the galaxy.

None of that mattered at the moment, though. One look and Minn-Erva shouted into her comm-link, "Incoming! Everyone, evac! Get out of that crater *now!*"

There was static on the other end, and then suddenly, *SKKAAARRRRR.* "—see it, right above! Korath and I are out!"

Then she looked down as the stealth bomb began its deadly dive to the surface, heading straight for the bunker. Closer to Minn-Erva, she could just see Att-Lass and Korath climbing up and over the edge of the crater. But what about the rest of the team?

The stealth bomb hit its target, and everything went white.

The scent of ozone hung in the air, and the white flash had been replaced with a thick black soot that descended from the sky like fallout. Minn-Erva had managed to avert her eyes right before impact, sparing herself the flash blindness usually caused by a stealth bomb. Static hissed and crackled over her comm-link as she tried to reach out to her teammates.

"Att-Lass, Korath, do you copy? Yon-Rogg, Bron-Char, do you copy?"

More static.

Minn-Erva pulled herself out of the rocky nook in which she'd been waiting and climbed over the top. Looking down, she couldn't see the concrete bunker, only the thick black soot as it fell. She felt a slight breeze behind her.

In a heartbeat, her body shifted, turned, and she had swiveled around, weapon slung into firing position. Her finger had tripped the switch from single shot to rapid-fire.

"Whoa! Whoa! It's us!"

Att-Lass.

She watched as he emerged from the soot, with Korath right next to him, a fine layer of dirt clinging to their persons.

"Any sign of Yon-Rogg or Bron-Char?" she asked.

Korath shook his head. "Nothing. Can you reach either of them on the comm-link?"

Minn-Erva opened her comm-link channel so Korath could hear the static. Korath nodded.

"What now?" Att-Lass said. "I say we go back down there and get Vers out of that bunker."

"We have our orders," Korath said, putting a hand on Att-Lass, who was already starting down the peak to the crater. "Back to the freighter. Now."

"Whose orders are those?" Minn-Erva asked.

"Yon-Rogg's. Straight from the top. We go

back to the freighter and wait. Bron-Char and Yon-Rogg can take care of themselves," Korath said.

"And Vers?" Minn-Erva pressed.

Korath paused for a moment and then shook his head. "Orders are orders. She can handle herself, too," he said.

For a moment, Minn-Erva even believed him.

CHAPTER 34

"What does *that* mean, 'I am the plans'?" Vers didn't make any effort to disguise her annoyance at Kaal's cryptic statement. She didn't have the time or patience to play games.

Peer Kaal smiled at Vers, but it didn't meet her eyes. "I am the plans. They are in my head. Only I know what they are," she said.

Vers looked at Peer Kaal. "Does it work?" she asked.

Kaal nodded slowly. "What you see on Sy'gyl is a direct result of the axiom cannon. Before the cannon, this planet was a paradise. Lush, dense forestry, plants and flowers of all kinds thriving, growing, taking root—and now?

The earthquakes. The fire. The lava flows. All of it."

"The axiom cannon did all this?" Vers said in disbelief.

"It is a terrible weapon," Kaal replied. "It destroys slowly, decimating a planet, until there's nothing left. Any greenery or plant life you see that's still surviving—if you were to return to Sy'gyl in a year, maybe less, there'd be nothing left."

Vers scratched the back of her head. "So if the plans are all in your head, I guess you're coming with me, then?"

Kaal reached inside her shirt as she walked over to Vers. Vers moved quickly, ready for an attack, but none came. "No, please, let me show you," Kaal said. Then Vers saw the silver chain that Kaal wore around her neck.

When she finished pulling out the chain, Vers saw something at the end of it. A small silver capsule, about the size of a bean. "I've recorded everything I know about the axiom cannon on this data capsule. Take it," Kaal said as she took the silver chain and handed it, along with the data capsule, to Vers.

Vers draped the chain around her neck, secreting it beneath her uniform, where no one would be able to see it. "What about you?" she said to Kaal. "What's gonna happen to you if you stick around?"

Kaal looked thoughtful. "I suppose when all is discovered, my treachery will be dealt with," she said, a sadness in her voice. "All I wanted to do was create. Now it has come to this." She gestured to the lab around her.

"Come with me," Vers said as she headed for the door. "We'll get you out of here."

"Go with the Kree? I think I like my chances better on Xandar," Kaal replied, a smile playing on her face. "No, you go. My place is here. Whatever my punishment, even if it be death, it is worth it knowing that there will be balance in the galaxy."

"You can have balance *now*!"

A voice from behind Vers had cried out, and before she could turn around, she felt it. Hot metal slicing into her right leg. Deep. The pain was blinding—in fact, it didn't even register as pain at first.

Instinctively, her hands reached out and grabbed at the edge of the knife, trying to knock it loose. The woman wielding the weapon was wearing Xandarian battle gear, and she was built like a wall. Vers slammed the hand that held the knife into the wall once, twice, three times.

The woman wouldn't release her hold.

"This is what happens to traitors!" the Xandarian shouted, struggling to free her hand from Vers's grip and attack Peer Kaal.

"Put. The knife. Down!" Vers grunted against the pain in her leg as she put all her might behind one more punch to the Xandarian's knife hand. The warrior dropped it at last, and the metal hit the floor with a loud clang.

And then there was a high-pitched whistling sound. . . .

"Incoming!" Vers shouted.

But by then, it was already too late. The bunker exploded around them, throwing Vers to the ground. In the explosion, she lost sight of Peer Kaal and the Xandarian warrior who had just tried to kill her.

CHAPTER 35

"It's hard to believe that any vegetation has stayed alive through these fires and lava," Dey observed quietly, drawing Vers back to the present as they made their way through the sparse forest.

They had been in the brush for about a half hour or so, Vers figured, putting some distance between them and the site of their skirmish with the Skrull. "Our ship's just beyond that stand of trees up there," she said, motioning with her head. "I think."

"My mission is to get you *to* your ship safe and sound," Dey said. "I don't have any desire to meet any of your crew. And I'm pretty sure they don't have any desire to meet me."

Vers looked at Dey. "You know something."

Dey seemed taken aback, and a little surprised. "Me? I know nothing. Ask anyone, they'll tell you," he said.

"Spill."

With a sigh, Dey started in. "You want to know why you were the one chosen to enter the compound and get the plans?"

Is this guy reading my mind?

"Because out of everyone on your team, you're the one who's least likely to kill first and ask questions later," Dey replied.

Vers didn't say anything, just kept walking. She heard the sound of hissing gas in the distance.

"Same reason you were chosen?" Vers asked.

Dey nodded. "Yep."

"How do you know?" Vers said. "Why should I believe you?"

"You don't have to believe me," Dey said. "I'm following orders, just like you. But this sort of mission doesn't just happen. It has to come down from the highest levels."

Highest levels? What does he mean?

"The two of you should have a whole army following you, for all the noise you're making."

Vers was interrupted from her furious train of thought by a voice erupting from behind the tree line.

"Yon-Rogg!" Vers called out. There he was, emerging from behind the trunk of a gnarled tree, with Bron-Char and Sun-Val behind him.

"You all made it, I see," Vers said drily.

"We followed the three Xandarians we saw back at the compound, made sure they didn't circle back, and gave you time to get the plans," Yon-Rogg said. "You did get the—?"

"What do you think?" Vers asked shortly.

Yon-Rogg smiled and held up his hands in a mock gesture of surrender. Then he turned to face Rhomann Dey. The smile faded away. "Your mission is completed," Yon-Rogg said.

Dey nodded. "She's all yours," he said. "A pleasure to never have met you, and know nothing about what happened here this day."

"Likewise," Yon-Rogg said.

"Thank you," Vers said, eyes meeting Dey's. "Great time."

"The best," Dey replied. Then he walked the opposite way. In less than a minute, he had disappeared into the thick woods.

"Better head back to the freighter," Sun-Val said, her voice taking on an urgent tone.

"What are you doing out here, Sun-Val?" Vers inquired. "Shouldn't you be with the freighter?"

"We found her in the forest on our way back," Bron-Char said. "Thought she saw something, so she left the freighter to investigate."

"Had to make sure no one was trying to hijack our ride," Sun-Val said.

Vers didn't buy it for a minute.

CHAPTER 36

They broke through the trees, and then it happened.

Vers emerged first, Sun-Val next to her, with Yon-Rogg and Bron-Char right behind. To Vers, it was like everything was playing out in slow motion.

Just ahead of them was the freighter. Vers saw Att-Lass standing by the hatch, and made out Korath in the cockpit. The ship's engines were humming, ready for blastoff. Minn-Erva was about halfway between the freighter and the trees, approaching Vers.

"Get down!" Minn-Erva shouted suddenly as she lowered her weapon, taking aim.

Is she trying to shoot me?

That's when Vers felt it: the barrel of a weapon shoved in between her shoulder blades, and heard Yon-Rogg and Bron-Char shout to her.

"Get down!"

Minn-Erva, again.

Vers fell to the ground, hitting the stone surface hard. She felt the impact on her injured leg, and then something tore.

From the ground, she saw Minn-Erva let loose with two shots.

Then Vers heard a body slump down next to her.

Sun-Val.

Only it wasn't Sun-Val. Her face slowly changed, twisting, morphing, until Vers knew exactly who and what the person was.

A Skrull. The other one Dey was talking about.

"Sun-Val. A Skrull?" Vers whispered, almost inaudibly.

"No," Minn-Erva said, approaching the

Skrull. She wasn't breathing. "Not Sun-Val. The real Sun-Val is dead. Killed by this one."

Att-Lass ran over from the hatch and knelt down next to Vers. "We found Sun-Val's body on the way back to the freighter. She must have been drawn out by the Skrull who killed her and took her place."

"Hoping to kill you and take the plans," Yon-Rogg said. "You really do have them?"

Reaching inside her uniform, Vers extricated the silver chain with the data capsule at the end and pulled it over her head, dropping it into Yon-Rogg's hand. "Got your plans right here," she said. With almost inhuman effort, Vers rose to her feet and made her way to the ship, willing herself not to pass out every step of the way.

CHAPTER 37

Vers listened to the loud humming of the freighter's engines. She tried to sit up, momentarily forgetting that her motion was restricted by two bands of cloth; one against her chest, the other restraining her legs. She looked down at her right leg, immobilized in a gel-like casing.

"Don't try to sit up," Minn-Erva said, sauntering over from where she had been watching over the freighter's auto-pilot controls. Luckily the course home was expected to be much smoother than the trip there, as they were now without Sun-Val. The loss of the talented pilot weighed heavily on the team, especially

Yon-Rogg, but in typical Kree warrior fashion the mission would be completed first. Emotions would come later. "You lost a lot of blood. Your leg's a mess."

"But I get to keep it, right?" Vers said, trying to smile.

"Yech, don't smile—that's gonna make me sick," Minn-Erva said. "You'll be fine. And you did all right, by the way," she added grudgingly. "You came through."

"So did you," Vers said, her throat scratchy.

"What did you expect?" Minn-Erva replied with a shrug. Then she got up and walked toward the cockpit.

⁕

"Good focus."

Yon-Rogg.

"Hey, boss," Vers said, trying to keep the tone of the conversation light.

"How's the leg?" he asked.

"I've had worse."

"Get some rest. When we reach the Kree

home world, you're heading straight for the med-bay," Yon-Rogg said.

"Yon-Rogg," Vers said, pulling on his sleeve. "Rhomann Dey said something while we were down there. About the mission."

"You know you can't trust a Xandarian," Yon-Rogg said. "Or believe anything they say."

"He tried to tell me why I was chosen for this mission. Why I was the one sent into the compound."

"And do you think he was telling you the truth?"

Vers was quiet. "I'm not sure," she said.

"Does it matter?"

With that, Yon-Rogg stood up, and left Vers to her thoughts.

Yes. Yes it does.